ABOARD THE GREAT IRON HORSE:

The

Clockwork God

By

JAMIE SEDGWICK

Look for these exciting titles by
Jamie Sedgwick:

The Tinkerer's Daughter steampunk series

*Aboard the Great Iron Horse steampunk
series*

*The Hank Mossberg Fantasy/Detective
Series*

The Shadow Born Trilogy

The Last Heist

&More!

Engineer's Log, Day 43

Today, we caught a glimpse of green vegetation erupting through the ice and many leagues to the south, the promising blue-green hue of what appears to be a forest. A rousing cheer went up among the residents of the *Iron Horse,* and I sounded the whistle in celebration. I have promised them a hunting trip as soon as we reach the woods. I admit feeling a certain sense of relief in this matter, as many of our supplies have run low and tensions have been high among the crew. At the outset, I made every effort to emphasize the importance of respect and cooperation in this adventure, but I have found certain crewmembers to be of intractable disposition and irrevocably set in their ways. I sense that at some point in the near future, we may have a reckoning.

We have been traveling for six weeks. After departing Sanctuary, our journey led us through the ancient subterranean tunnels built under the city almost a thousand years ago. Upon reaching a sheer wall of solid ice at the end of the tunnels, I ordered the crew to secure our cargo, and we rammed through at full speed. It was the exact sort of task *the Horse* was built for, though the exercise seemed to put my crew through considerable emotional strain. When they realized that we were barreling full-steam into a wall of ice, a few of them actually panicked. Thankfully, no one was hurt, and the ice provided little resistance to the *Horse's* hardened steel chassis.

After breaking through, we were disheartened to learn that we were still buried under at least thirty feet of snow. We pressed on at half speed, tunneling in darkness for three days, catching only occasional glimpses of filtered sunlight shining down in a bluish hue from above. Several crewmembers suffered from the irrational fear of claustrophobia, and I had to sedate one man with a tea of powdered duskwood leaves. Then, at last, the tracks rose to meet the frozen steppes of the Wastelands, and we once again saw the sun. Unfortunately, in the Wastelands there is little else to see. The crew quickly grew demoralized at the sight of endless miles of snow and ice, and within hours, they were back to quarreling.

Since that day, we have glimpsed occasional herds of caribou, wolves and bear, as well as wild hare and a variety of raptors and field mice, almost all of which are cloaked in white fur or feathers that undoubtedly aid their survival in this desolate landscape. We have also encountered and befriended a diminutive humanoid creature by the name of Micah, who has since taken up residence in the attic over the library and proclaimed himself the train's cartographer. He came prepared with maps of territories that we have not yet explored, and I hope that his talents will prove valuable to our expedition.

To his credit, Micah is not only quite artistic, but has also proven popular among the crew. They seem to enjoy his jokes and the improbable stories of his adventures. I am thankful for his presence if for no other reason than it seems to have -temporarily at least- put an end to the brawling.

Jamie Sedgwick

Chapter 1

"I'll show three fools if you have a king," Kale announced, leaning precariously back in his chair, a twisted smile pulling up the corners of his mouth. Smoldering blue eyes gazed out from under dark bangs, the tips of his hair just grazing the angry red scar on his right cheek. Kale tossed his head, and as he did, the old wooden chair frame creaked under the sinewy warrior's great weight. River glanced at Kale over her cards, ignoring the man's hardened muscles and deep penetrating gaze, searching for the telltale curl of his lips that always belied a bluff. In response, he shot her a devious grin.

He's getting better at this, she thought grimly.

The other occupants of the dining car watched in silence as the players examined their hands, the endless drone of the rails filling their ears, the low humming sound punctuated by the occasional *clinking* of dishes and the *creaking* noise of the *Horse's* massive steel chassis. Outside, the barren landscape seemed almost motionless. It was a world frozen, static, entirely lacking anything that resembled comfort, warmth, or safety. Endless fields of prairie stretched out in every direction, marked only by bright rivers of snow and scattered piles of boulders. Far to the north, barely visible in the haze, rose the sharp craggy peaks of distant mountains. A few leagues ahead and out of sight to the occupants of the *Iron*

Horse, spread a massive forest. This they hoped, signaled a change in their fortunes.

"Fool's a bet," River said at last, pursing her full, pouty lips. She threw a handful of copper coins on the table. "I call your hand."

"I'm out," said Burk, the tall bald-headed blacksmith. He scratched his thick black beard as he tossed his cards on the table. "Someone buy me a drink!"

"Me too," said one of the other players, tossing his cards aside. River grinned with satisfaction as the other players abandoned the game. At last, only River and Kale remained. In unison, the two players spread their cards on the table, face up.

"Three kings!" River exclaimed, her eyes widening as she stared at Kale's cards. She fixed the warrior with a hard stare. "You lied!"

"Bluffed," he said with a wink. "I bluffed, just like I always do. Why do you keep falling for it?"

River snarled as Kale leaned forward to gather the stack of coins from the table. They were mostly copper, but a few silvers had found their way into the pot. For a moment, it looked like River might take a swing at him. The crowd around them went tense. They had seen River fight before. Kale however, didn't flinch. He'd known River since she was a babe and there weren't many things he could do that would drive her to violence. If he knew a sure way, he'd do it more often. He enjoyed a good wrestling match with a beautiful woman.

Deep down, Kale was absolutely certain that River was madly in love with him. Why wouldn't she be? He was the best looking man on the *Horse* by far, and she was... well, she was River. Her blonde hair and fine skin were the stuff of legends. She was gorgeous. And, in Kale's opinion, the universe had put the two of them together for a reason. It was just a matter of time until she came to her senses and figured that out. Until then, he'd just let nature take its course...

"All hands, dead stop!" a voice shouted over the communications pipe, and the train's whistle blew furiously. At the same moment, the brakes locked up. A horrible grinding, screeching noise came up from the wheels, and the floor of the dining car began to vibrate. The table bounced forward, slamming into River's chest and knocking her to the ground. At the same time, Kale's chair leapt into the air and dumped him unceremoniously to the floor. All around them, people slammed into walls and furniture. Glasses, plates, and bottles crashed to the floor and shattered. Kale's precious stack of coppers scattered from one end of the dining car to the other.

The *Iron Horse* quickly lost speed and the sudden loss of momentum made it all but impossible for the untrained crew to regain their footing. The elf-like Tal'mar were first to get back on their feet. Their slender builds and agility allowed them to negotiate the tsunami of broken glass and overturned furniture while their heavier human counterparts were still floundering. They lunged for the door and vanished up the brass ladders to the rooftops. River, Kale, and the others were still scrambling to find footing without slicing open a vein on the broken glass.

At last, the screeching subsided and the train's whistle went mute. Gradually, inch by inch, the *Iron*

Horse rolled to a stop. The last of the crew abandoned the train, leaping out onto the frozen ground. They scanned the tracks ahead and immediately discerned the problem. A pile of boulders the size of a house lay across the southern set of tracks.

Kale and River rushed up to the locomotive and found Socrates perched on the railing near the front smokestacks, looking down over the scene with a frown. Socrates was the chief engineer and commander of the expedition. From a distance, Socrates could easily have passed for a simple primate, but up close, he was something entirely different. In reality, Socrates was an autonomous gorilla powered by steam. His body was covered in dense blue-black fur. Open patches in the fur on the side of his head and one forearm revealed tiny, intricate mechanisms of brass and copper gears, cogs, and machinery. A small smokestack poked up behind his ear, releasing puffs of steam at regular intervals. Standing there on the platform wearing his leather vest and rectangular tinted glasses, the simian looked almost human.

Socrates caught hold of the brass bar mounted near the stairs and swung himself deftly off the platform. He vaulted through the air and thumped to the ground heavily behind River and Kale. They watched in silence as he lumbered past, the machinery inside of him clicking and whirring ever so quietly. The rest of the crew parted to make way for their leader. Socrates circled the pile of stones on the tracks, touching them here and there, making calculations in his head. He stepped back to stare at the boulders, scratching his chin. This went on for several minutes, until at last he turned to face the crewmembers who had gathered at the front of the locomotive.

"We can't clear the tracks by hand," he said in a booming voice. "We'll have to assemble the crane. Burk, I'll need your help with that. I'll also need you, River. The rest of you, start cleaning up the mess. Kale, take someone back to the fifth cargo car and unload the steamwagon. We'll need it to haul the crane." Kale tapped a nearby Tal'mar man on the shoulder and they both took off. The rest of the crew grumbled as they went to work, but not enough to get Socrates' attention.

River and Burk followed Socrates back to one of the many massive cargo cars a few hundred yards down the train. An icy wind splashed over them as they walked, and the frozen ground crunched under their feet. Somewhere in the distance, a wolf howled and a moment later, a second responded.

"To think we left Sanctuary for this," Burk said as he rubbed the goose bumps on his arms. "Nothin' but dead grass and snow as far as the eye can see. I'm startin' to think the whole world's a wasteland."

"There are signs of life all around you," Socrates said as he climbed the ladder and released the latch on the railcar. "If you simply open your eyes to them. Look, a raptor flying over the hill there, closing in on a field mouse or hare, no doubt."

Burk snorted and rolled his eyes. "You and I got diff'rent ideas about life, I think."

Socrates shoved the door open. It rolled to the side, rumbling and squeaking as the rusty bearings came to life for the first time in centuries. Pale afternoon light washed into the railcar, revealing a cargo of steel pipes, trusses, and brackets, all neatly ordered but covered by dust and cobwebs. Socrates swung himself inside and thumped down heavily on the wooden floor, sending a cloud of dust floating through the air. River reached up, latching onto the edge of the floor, and pulled herself into the car. Burk grumbled as he climbed up the ladder to join them.

It took Socrates a few hours to sort out the pieces and get them organized. As he did this, River and Burk loaded the parts onto the steamwagon, and then began to erect the crane. Sometime during this process, Micah appeared. In physical appearance, it would have been easy to mistake the halfling for a child. He had a thin build and stood at just under three feet in height, but his long pointed chin, crooked nose, and sharp green eyes belied a much older and wiser, highly intelligent being. Micah was dressed warmly with a long wool jacket, scarf, and gloves. He wore a short, rounded hat with a wide, crooked brim, and he carried a walking stick in one hand. He had a leather satchel thrown over his shoulder. No one noticed the small, imp-like creature until he stood up straight and cleared his throat. They all turned at once.

"Good morning, cartographer," Socrates said, looking him up and down. "I gather you're going on a hike."

"I'd like to make some sketches, possibly start a new map," Micah said, patting his satchel. "If you don't mind, that is."

Socrates glanced at the barren hills stretching out behind the train. "I suppose there's no harm in it. Perhaps it would be wise to bring a companion along though, considering we have no idea what manner of creatures might roam these plains."

"I'll go!" Kale said. They twisted their heads around to see the stocky warrior sitting on top of the railcar, looking down at them. River narrowed her eyebrows.

"How long have you been up there?"

Kale smiled wickedly. "Not long enough."

River raised her fist at him, but Socrates was quick to intervene. "Excellent idea, Kale. Grab a musket and take an herb bag with you. Our stocks are running low, and it seems our next hunt will be delayed. See what you can gather, or kill."

"My pleasure," Kale said. He disappeared down the ladder and vanished inside the train. Socrates turned to find River staring at him. He could see from the look on her face that she wanted to join Kale and Micah. Despite all of their bickering and fighting, Socrates knew the two youths were true friends, going all the way back to childhood. At times, they were almost like siblings. He gave her a sympathetic look, or as close to it as his simian features allowed.

"I'm afraid I can't let you go, River. You're my only mechanic, and I need you here."

"I understand," she said, sighing. "Just promise I'll get to stretch my legs soon. I've been cramped up in this train for weeks."

"We all have," Burk said in a gruff voice. "The sooner we get our work done, the sooner we get a rest."

River cocked an eyebrow at him. "Who said anything about resting, old man?"

"Careful girl, I'm not *that old,*" he said. "Here, unhitch this truss, would you?"

River laughed as she snatched up a wrench. She threw herself into her work, ignoring Kale and Micah who were disappearing over the hill. She couldn't help feeling a twinge of jealousy, but River knew she had to do her part to keep the train running. After all, this journey wasn't just about a simple adventure. It was about saving Socrates' life. And perhaps thousands of others.

Socrates -along with most of the technology from Sanctuary- was based on a rare element known as Starfall. It was the source of power for their steam technology and without it, all civilization might be in danger. And without a new supply of Starfall, Socrates would die. That was why the *Iron Horse* had set out in the first place. But in the meanwhile, River was looking forward to seeing something besides ice and snow. She'd had her fill of the cold. She wanted to see green land and blue mountains, maybe even an ocean. And something else, too. River was looking for something. She wasn't sure what it was yet, but she felt it every time she looked towards the horizon. Something out there was calling her, and she intended to find out what it was.

Chapter 2

Micah waited for Kale atop the hill overlooking the *Iron Horse.* He was smoking a pipe with a long, sharply curved brass stem and a clay bowl shaped into the likeness of the mythical *woodsman,* an old man with a wizened face and a long beard that curved down around the base of the bowl. As Micah waited, puffing absent-mindedly on his pipe, he sketched out the scene before him on a rough piece of parchment. The landscape was forlorn and barren, lacking any form of warmth or comfort. The *Horse's* rails cut through the frozen earth like a scar stretching into the distance, the cold black steel formidable and unforgiving and somehow fitting in that harsh, bleak environment.

Up from the rails rose the shape of the *Iron Horse,* a mass of soot-blackened steel and brass and copper pipes gleaming against black paint, thick columns of smoke rising from the smokestacks along the massive boiler to mingle with the cloud-darkened skies looming overhead. It was a dark scene overall, an image of impending doom and harsh contrasts, and to Micah's eye, absolutely stunning. It was a moment he felt compelled to capture.

Micah heard Kale approaching -the sound of his tall boots crunching across the frozen ground, his long blue cloak flapping wildly in the breeze- and hurried to finish the sketch. Moments later, satisfied that the bones of the image at least were in place,

Micah rolled up the parchment, tucked it safely into his satchel, and glanced up at his companion. Kale wore a massive broadsword with a gleaming silver pommel strapped to his back and clutched a flute-barreled musket in one hand and a light travel bag in the other. Micah also noted that Kale wore a broad smile on his face. His companion, it seemed, was anxious for an adventure.

Kale joined Micah on the hilltop and took a long look at the surrounding landscape. He drew his gaze along the railroad tracks racing into the distance, and saw the barely visible line of woods rising out of the earth. His heart leapt at the sight. Like the others, Kale had been trapped aboard the *Iron Horse* far too long. He *needed* to see what was in those woods.

"Not much around here," Kale said, choosing his words carefully, hoping to guide his companion to a certain conclusion. "All plains and snow. Probably not a plant or animal for miles."

"Except what lies ahead," Micah said cleverly. "Perhaps we should scout up the tracks and take a peek into that forest. For the others, you know. Make sure they won't be running into any more trouble."

"My thoughts exactly," Kale said with a smile. He shouldered the musket, adjusting it so it wouldn't interfere with his broadsword, and then pulled his cloak tight around his shoulders. He started down the hill, intentionally choosing a path that took them out of sight of the train, and Micah fell in next to him, somehow matching the much larger man's pace even as he pulled out another sheet of parchment and began sketching the landscape ahead. Every minute or so, the small fellow dipped his quill into an inkpot attached to his satchel. Kale noticed that his companion switched hands from time to time, hardly missing a beat as he continued to draw and walk at the same time.

"How do you do that?" Kale said at some point.

"Do what?" Micah said absently, staring at his sketch.

"How can you draw with both hands? I can't even draw with one."

"I don't know," Micah said. "I was the only one in my village with this ability. Then again, I was also the only artist. Perhaps it just takes practice."

"Maybe," said Kale, wishing it was true. He'd have given anything to swing a broadsword left-handed with the same dexterity as his right. No amount of practice would ever change the reality that his right arm was stronger and more agile. "What was your village like?"

Micah paused in his sketching for a moment, and then quickly resumed before he began to speak:

"Small. So small, compared to the rest of the world. We lived on the ridge of a mountain in huts and tree houses. We farmed what we could from the land, which wasn't much. The soil was rocky and infertile. We lived mostly off of wild berries and small game."

"Why did you leave?"

Micah sighed. "Because there was no reason to stay," he said in a melancholy voice.

Kale narrowed his eyebrows. "A woman?" he said suspiciously.

Micah glanced at him, and went back to his sketching. Kale took the silence that followed as a sign that his line of questioning had become too personal. He also assumed it meant he was correct, but he was smart enough to drop the subject.

"How about that scar?" Micah said, nodding towards the angry red mark on Kale's cheek. "Is that the work of a jealous husband, or lover?"

Kale subconsciously reached up to touch the scar. The skin was hard there, callused like the hands of a blacksmith, but still red as if it had happened yesterday. "It was a Vangar spear," he said.

"A spear? That looks like a burn to me."

"It is. The spear hit a boiler I was standing next to. The pain was so bad I blacked out. I was twelve years old. It was the same year the Vangars killed my family."

"I've heard stories of them, from the crew. You're lucky to be alive."

"So they say," Kale said distantly. He drew his gaze to the north, his sharp eyes scanning the surrounding hills for signs of game, but also for any hint of danger. Kale knew well enough that many wild beasts had natural camouflaging abilities that made them all but invisible until they were within striking distance. He had learned to always be wary. Despite his brazen attitude, Kale had a healthy respect for the dangers of the wilds.

The two men pressed on, falling silent for a time. After putting a good distance between themselves and the train, Micah put his drawings away. The treetops were still no more than a thin line of green on the horizon.

"Shall we run?" Kale said. "We'd make better time. If you're up for it, that is."

Micah closed his satchel and broke into a sprint. "Just try to keep up!" he called over his shoulder. Kale laughed and took off after him. It didn't take long for Kale to realize that Micah may have been small, but he could bound across the steppes like a prairie rabbit. To his surprise, Kale did indeed find himself struggling to keep up. Of course, Kale had a good deal more weight to carry. Not only was he several times the size of his companion, but the broadsword on his back probably weighed as much as Micah. Kale also had the long, poorly balanced musket to contend with. It wasn't long before Kale was huffing and puffing, trying quite seriously just to keep pace, while Micah sprinted ahead tirelessly. Kale pressed on, not about to be outdone by a man less than half his height.

They crossed two leagues of rolling hills and scattered patches of snow in this manner, until they finally came within sight of a river lined with weeping willows and birch trees. Beyond, dense evergreens closed in, and the forest grew thick and dark. To the north, a hill swept up towards a smooth plateau.

"Let's climb up there," Micah said, pointing at the plateau. "I can make a quick sketch of the landscape for my map."

Kale glanced at the sun. It had passed directly overhead while they were running, and was now beginning its slide toward the horizon. "We won't make it back to the train before nightfall even if we leave now," he said. "I guess we'll be traveling by the stars tonight. All right... we'll take a quick hike up the hill, but I'm only stopping long enough for a meal."

"Agreed," Micah said happily. "Very wise decision."

"Why is that?"

"Because you agree with me! There's no surer measure of a man's intellect." Kale couldn't help laughing as Micah shouldered his satchel and started the climb. Fortunately, it was a relatively short hike to the top, and in a few minutes, they had approached the summit. Kale stopped short when he noticed a wrought iron fence rising out of the hill ahead. He drew the musket from his shoulder and motioned for Micah to remain silent as they proceeded forth. As they neared the top, they were surprised to see tall stone and marble grave markers rising out of the earth.

"It's a graveyard," Micah said. He turned slowly, scanning the surrounding countryside. "There's nothing else here. Where did it come from?"

"It's old," Kale observed. "Maybe from before the cataclysm."

The place was in a terrible state of disrepair. Many of the stones had toppled over, and the sepulchers had collapsed inward under their own weight. In other places the graves looked sunken, as if the coffins had rotted away to nothing, leaving empty spaces in the earth beneath. The rows of grave markers stretched out across the plateau for several hundred yards, separated here and there by dark pathways overgrown with scrub brush and sage, and terminated by tall, ominous looking crypts.

"There's something odd about this place," Micah said. "It feels *haunted*."

"It's your imagination," said Kale. "It's just a graveyard, that's all."

Kale wouldn't admit it of course, but he had also noticed something unusual about the place. Not just the fact that it was an ancient ruin or a resting place for the dead, but an eerie sensation that he was being watched. It was as if the ghosts from ages past still lurked in the shadows of those tombs and crypts. He approached the tall wrought iron gates, sword at the ready. The hairs were standing on the back of his neck, but Kale wasn't about to show a hint of fear. Micah had frozen in his tracks several yards back.

"Maybe we shouldn't go in there," Micah said quietly behind him. "You know, sacred ground and all. Wouldn't want the uh, the spirits to take offense."

Kale was inclined to agree, but his thirst for adventure had a hold of him and it was too late to back down now without looking a coward. "Wait here," he said over his shoulder. "I'm just taking a quick look around."

"Be careful," Micah said.

The tall wrought iron gate creaked ominously as Kale pushed through and stepped inside. A forest of headstones and ancient, decaying statues rose up before him. All around, he saw signs of rot and neglect. Bits and pieces of ancient text appeared here and there on the stones, but they were worn beyond legibility and many were covered in the moss and the overgrowth of centuries. He heard the sound of his companion's footsteps retreating to the edge of the plateau, and a grim smile came to his lips. He pressed on.

23

A tall statue of a woman appeared up ahead. She wore long robes and had fine, straight hair that fell over her worn features. Her neck bent forward so that her face seemed to frown down over those who passed by on the trail beneath her. Kale felt a strange sadness as he glanced up at her face. He couldn't help but think the statue had been modeled after a real woman; a woman who had long since succumbed to death's dark grasp. There was a sorrow in her face so real and tangible that Kale was sure the woman had lived a hard life, and lost everyone she loved. It almost seemed that if he stared long enough, the stone might come to life and begin weeping.

He slipped past, telling himself it was all his imagination. Kale pushed his way through the scrub brush and eventually came to a tall crypt covered with ivy and moss. Grotesque, demonic faces leered down at him from atop the marble pillars, and recessed beams framed the heavy iron doors. The doors stood partially open, and Kale noted the broken sections of iron chain lying scattered on the ground before them.

He stood there a moment, gathering his courage, feeling the weight of the musket in his hands. The thought flashed through his mind that this building may have been turned into a lair by some wild and dangerous creature. Kale's only companion was beyond shouting distance, and would be of no help in a dire situation. By the time the crew of the *Iron Horse* learned of his fate, it would already be too late. It would be foolhardy to venture into such a place under those conditions.

"Foolhardy indeed," Kale murmured as he stepped up to the threshold and shouldered the door open wide enough to allow him entrance.

Chapter 3

Micah didn't like Kale leaving him alone in that place. He could sense evil spirits and wandering ghosts of the dead all around him. Every gust of the cold north wind sent a chill down his spine, and he started at the sounds of quivering branches and leaves blowing across the tombs. Still, it was better to be there, outside the graveyard, than joining his companion on the mad quest *into* the tombs.

Micah and his kind had a healthy respect for the dead, and for all the wandering spirits of the world. Unlike humans and Tal'mar, who believed the spirits of the dead simply passed on to another world, Micah's race believed their ghosts remained to wander the world until they found the chance to be born again into a new mortal flesh. Disrespecting such creatures and their resting places was taboo of the highest order. So Micah wandered back to the edge of the plateau to wait, restlessly watching Kale delve deeper and deeper into that ghostly cemetery. When it became apparent that Kale wasn't going to return right away, Micah finally remembered the reason he'd climbed the hill in the first place. He settled down cross-legged on the ground, facing north with his back to the creepy graveyard, and opened his satchel. He produced several good quality parchments and began sketching the layout of the land along the railroad tracks, all the way up to the river and into the woods.

Micah's work absorbed him, and a few minutes later he had almost completely forgotten where he was. Kale was but a distant thought in the back of his mind. It was the *lines* that drew him in. Micah couldn't help being absorbed by them. He saw the way they formed the landscape, the way the river cut through the earth and the trees thrust up toward the heavens. He saw the shadows stretching out across blades of grass...

Micah heard a noise behind him. He snapped his head around, staring into the shadowy corners of the cemetery's undergrowth. He noticed suddenly that it was getting dark, and wondered how long he'd been drawing. It couldn't have been that long. He was only on his third sketch. He scanned the area, searching for any sign of movement, straining to hear another noise.

"Kale?" he said quietly. "Is that you?"

No response, other than a slight rustle of leaves in the breeze.

Micah rose to his feet and glanced at the sky. He noticed with some trepidation that the sun had moved halfway down towards the horizon. Already, shadows were growing long. He hastily rolled up his drawings and tucked them back in his satchel. He settled back down on the ground, this time facing the eerie necropolis.

Micah stared into the shadows for a while, watching and waiting, desperately hoping Kale would come walking out with that stupid grin on his face and say something like, "Did I scare you?" When that didn't happen, Micah once again turned to the only thing that could settle the anxiousness in the pit of his belly. He produced a fresh parchment and began sketching the graveyard.

Micah's sharp eyes gathered the angles and shadows, and the rugged, tilting lines of the tombstones. He hastily sketched out the tall, rectangular shapes looming over him and then captured the pieces of grave markers lying broken on the ground. He sketched in the ghastly faces carved into the crypts and sepulchers, and then began working on the ivy and scrub brush, and the nearly invisible pathways leading through the maze of tombs.

The distant ringing sound of steel on stone sent a chill crawling up his spine. Micah rose to his feet, staring into the lengthening shadows. He heard a human outcry in the distance, followed by the sound of something large and powerful tearing through the underbrush. Up ahead, the branches shook and rattled on the trail.

Micah took an unconscious step back, and stumbled as he tripped over his satchel. He fell backwards, landing hard on his rump. At that very moment, Kale burst out of the bushes.

"Run!" he shouted, his eyes wild with panic. "Run for your life!"

Kale's face was white as a sheet. He flew out through the cemetery gates and past Micah, waving his sword wildly in the air with both hands. The musket was nowhere to be seen.

Micah struggled to his feet and scrambled to gather the maps and parchments that had spilled out of his bag. Frantically, he shoved the papers back inside. He turned to run after Kale, but then paused. Somehow, curiosity got the best of him. Micah turned and squinted into the darkness under the brush around the tombs, wondering what manner of thing might have so frightened his heroic companion. He saw nothing. No movement, no flashes of light or color. He didn't hear anything either, except for the distant footfalls of Kale's boots as he went charging down the hillside.

A distant moaning sound echoed through the graveyard. It was like the sound of a tree swaying in the night, or the wind moaning through the eaves. Was it his imagination? Micah couldn't tell. The sound was so faint, so ethereal... The branches rustled slightly, but the movement was hardly noticeable. Certainly it was no more than a breeze.

Was that what had frightened Kale so? Micah thought. *A breeze in the branches?* A smile swept over Micah's features, and he took a step closer. He heard the moan again, soft and distant, and he laughed.

"Kale!" he called over his shoulder. "You fool, you've run away from a breeze! Get back here!"

He took a step towards the gate, reaching up to touch the cold wrought iron bars. As he did, a shape stirred in the brush. Suddenly, a tall humanlike creature burst out of the foliage and came lurching towards him. Micah's jaw dropped open. His eyes bulged and his heart hammered in his chest. He froze, one hand still clinging to the gate, the other desperately wringing the strap of his leather satchel at his shoulder. Terrified as he was, Micah couldn't move. A panicked cry slid from his lips, an attempt to scream that fizzled into little more than a whimper.

A few yards away, the lumbering creature caught sight of him and headed directly for Micah.

Behind it came another, and then another. They were hideous, more like corpses than humans, with rotting flesh and empty eye sockets. Their clothes were worn and disheveled, as if they had been rotting in those crypts for decades, and parts of their bodies had rotted away to the bone.

A heavy hand thumped down on Micah's shoulder and a terrified *"squeak!"* erupted from his lips. He slapped at his opponent, but Kale caught him by the wrists and spun the smaller man around to face him.

"I. Said. Run!" Kale shouted at him. He lifted Micah from the ground and tossed the diminutive man over his shoulder like a sack of potatoes. Micah could do little more than cling desperately to his satchel as Kale took off at a sprint down the hill. They flew to the base of the plateau, dashing into the shelter of the willows along the riverbank.

Kale paused there to catch his breath and return his companion to the earth. As one, they turned to stare back towards the hill. In the distance, they saw dark silhouettes of human corpses lurching down the slope.

"Devils! They're not stopping," Micah said breathlessly. "We have to run."

Kale spun around, surveying the river.

"It's too wide to cross here. And with our luck, those things can probably swim."

"Up there," Micah said, pointing in the direction of the railroad tracks. "I think I see a bridge." Kale squinted into the shadows, nodding silently.

"All right then, let's move. They're bound to lose our trail eventually."

They took off at a run, bounding through the brush and undergrowth, leaping fallen trees and branches. Micah easily paced his companion in this terrain. He was quite adept at running and leaping through the forest. Shortly, they reached the area where the railroad tracks plunged into the woods. There they found a train bridge with steel girders and trusses, and alongside it a wooden footbridge just wide enough for a wagon. The companions wasted no time crossing the footbridge. They went racing down the road beyond, into the shadows under the dense forest canopy, not even pausing to look back.

By the time they had run out of breath, the forest had closed in around them and the railroad tracks had disappeared somewhere off to their left. Kale slowed to a jog and then stopped. He found a good-sized stump alongside the road and thumped down, his massive chest heaving, streams of sweat running down his face. Micah leaned up against the stump next to him, pressing his forehead against the cool, damp, moss-covered wood.

"Think they're gone?" Micah said breathlessly, his voice muffled by the moss.

Kale had his eyes fixed on the road, and he didn't blink as he responded. "If we haven't lost them by now, we never will."

"Pleasant thought." Micah pushed away from the stump and walked to the center of the road. He settled down on the ground, staring back the way had come. "Do you think we should go back?"

That was enough to draw Kale's gaze back to his companion. He stared at Micah a moment, pondering the question. "I'm not going back there until daylight," he said. "Maybe not even then."

Micah nodded, tilting his head to the side. "Then it seems we have two choices. We can make camp for the night, or keep walking... *the other way.* We might eventually cross the tracks again. We can wait for the *Horse* there."

Kale pulled his gaze away from Micah to stare down the narrow road. A thought occurred to him.

"This is a traveled road," he said absently.

"Huh?"

"Look at the ground. No undergrowth, no shrubs. Somebody still uses this road."

"You're right! That means we're close to a city!"

"Maybe. Let's not get our hopes up. But if I know anything about those creatures back there, it's that they'll stay away from well-traveled roads."

Micah frowned. "Kale, what do you *know* about those creatures?"

"Nothing," Kale admitted. "I've never seen anything like that in my life."

"I've heard of it, in legends," Micah said. "The dead rise from their graves if you disturb their rest. Sometimes to seek justice."

"It wasn't me that disturbed them. Someone had already broken the chains on that crypt."

"Something is wrong with that place," Micah said with a shiver.

"There's nothing else for it," Kale said. "Not 'til dawn." He opened his bag and pulled out a loaf of bread, along with some dried venison and slightly moldy cheese. Micah gave him an incredulous look.

"How can you think of eating at a time like this? After what we just saw?" His burly companion shrugged.

"Learn to eat when you can," he said, "or risk not eating at all."

Micah considered that and realized there was a certain logic to it. "Now that you mention it, I am a bit hungry."

Kale divided the portions and handed Micah his share. He took a big bite of bread and chewed it slowly. "I should've brought a canteen. To think we're this close to the river and not a drop to drink. I need it, after that run."

Micah fumbled around in his bag for a moment and produced a small wineskin. "Will this do?" he said, displaying it to his companion. Kale grinned broadly.

"My friend, you can join me on a hunt any time you like."

Micah doubled over, laughing so hard he could hardly catch his breath. Kale watched him curiously, wondering if he'd just been insulted. At last, Micah straightened himself out with a sigh.

"And just what do you find so amusing?" Kale said with a narrow grin.

"I just remembered what we were supposed to be doing. I'd forgotten the whole reason for our hike was so that you could hunt."

"So much for that," Kale said. "I guess you were right. I never should have gone into that tomb."

"Just out of curiosity... what did you see in there?"

Kale stared into the distance, recalling the images in his memory. "The crypt was huge. At the bottom of the stairs, it opened up into a massive cave filled with coffins. I had my flint and steel handy, so I lit a torch and went inside to look around. The first thing I noticed was that a lot of the coffins had been opened. I looked inside a few, and they were empty. While I was looking around, I heard a noise up ahead and thought I saw a flash of light, so I went to investigate. That's when I turned a corner and found myself face-to-face with those... *things*."

"So those creatures we saw... they truly were the dead, then?"

"I only know what my eyes saw."

"Trust your eyes then," said Micah. "I saw them, too."

Micah shuddered and turned his head as if he could turn away from the haunting visions in his mind. He took a swig from the wineskin and fixed his gaze on Kale. "I was just wondering, why didn't you just kill those creatures with that huge sword of yours? You seem to know how to handle a weapon."

"Don't think I didn't try. I hacked one's arm off and he just kept coming. He didn't even feel it. So I hacked off his leg. The thing fell down on the ground and came crawling after me. You have to take off their heads. By the time I figured that out, there were just too many."

Micah licked his lips dryly. "I see... just *how many* were there?"

Kale took a big bite of jerked meat. "You don't want to know," he said around his food.

Micah stared at him. "Kale, what happened to your musket?"

"I dropped it in the tomb. Never got a shot off. Just as well, I suppose. I think noise attracts their attention."

Micah took a swig from the wineskin and stared back down the road anxiously. "Socrates won't like that," he muttered.

"Then Socrates can go get it," Kale grumbled.

Chapter 4

River and her companions spent the rest of the afternoon and most of the evening assembling the crane, and then maneuvering it into place along the tracks. By then it was dark, and Socrates called for a dinner break. The cook and his helpers had set up collapsible tables outside the dining car so to serve the crew under the open sky. They lit the area with a few torches and a small bonfire that offered comfort and light, though neither were truly necessary. The flickering firelight gave the area a pleasant ambiance, but the wind had died down and the moon was already high in the sky, and nearly full.

What lifted their moods most was when Socrates thumped a keg of ale down on one of the tables and hammered a tap into it. A cheer went up all around the camp. A line immediately formed, and Socrates began filling their tankards. Before long, the somber mood had lifted and the air was buzzing with lively conversations. A few of the workers even broke out singing while they drank.

River wasn't fond of ale and cared even less for standing in line. She helped herself to a steaming bowl of stew and a freshly baked dinner roll, and joined Burk who was sitting alone at one of the tables. The older man had already finished his meal as well as his first tankard of ale. He was eyeing the line at the keg as River settled down across the table.

"Your friend must have run into trouble," Burk said as she joined him. "He's still not back."

River glanced around the area and realized Burk was talking about Kale.

"He probably wandered further than he meant to," she said. "Knowing Kale, he'll sleep under the stars tonight and we'll have to hold the train up in the morning because he overslept."

Burk laughed. "Kale left with Micah. The little one might convince him to come back tonight."

"Don't count on it. Kale's as stubborn as a mule and twice as lazy. If Micah comes back tonight, he'll come back alone."

"I doubt that'll happen," said Burk. "The little one's scared of his own shadow."

"Maybe."

"Maybe? Don't tell me you haven't noticed, Micah's as skittish as a field mouse."

River leaned forward on her elbows. "Of course I have. But I keep thinking about where we found him, hundreds of miles from nowhere, all alone in the Wastes. If we hadn't stopped to hunt those deer, we wouldn't even have found Micah. If it had been any one of us, they'd have found a frozen corpse. Micah might be small, but it takes something special to survive alone in the Wastes like that. I know, I've made the journey from the Blackrocks to Sanctuary on foot. I think there's more to him than meets the eye."

Burk stroked his beard. "From what I heard, he came from a village in the east Blackrocks. It does take some daring to get that far alone. Or at least some proper motivation."

"Motivation? What do you mean by that?"

Burk leaned closer and lowered his voice.

"Maybe he *wasn't* alone."

"What are you saying?"

"Maybe he just *ended up alone*, if you know what I mean."

River raised an eyebrow and grinned slightly. "Are you implying he killed someone?"

"Just thinkin' aloud," Burk said, leaning back. "For instance, why would the little fellow run so far from home, all alone like that? Maybe he left his troubles behind, that's why."

"So now you have him running away from a crime? That's a lot of speculation, Burk," River said. "Maybe Micah was just working on his maps and got lost. Wouldn't that make more sense?"

"It might," Burk said with a wicked grin, "but it ain't near as much fun. Besides, it's good to know where we stand with our mates. Now, take old Socrates for example: *What's his motivation?*"

River frowned. "We already know what his motivation is. He needs more Starfall, or he'll die. You might say the same for the rest of us, considering. Look how dependent we are on steam power now. We weren't like that before. If we lose our energy source now, I'd wager that thousands will die the first winter."

"Aye, perhaps, perhaps. But if you ask me, Socrates was in a awful hurry to get out of Sanctuary. Makes you wonder what they'll find when they start going through all those big empty buildings back in the city, doesn't it? Maybe they're not so empty, eh?"

"Not at all," River said, laughing. "I already explored some of them. Tell me Burk, what do *you* think they'll find?"

He shrugged and tipped his tankard back, patiently waiting for the last drop of ale to fall on his tongue. "Maybe they'll find out what *really happened* to all the people that used to live in that city," he said, gazing up into the empty container.

"You've put a lot of thought into this conspiracy theory, haven't you?"

"I've had a lot of time to think. Ain't nothin' else to do on this damn train."

"Have you been talking about this with the others?"

"Hasn't been nothin' else to do, 'cept play cards and drink. But Socrates won't let us have more than one drink a day, and I ran out of money weeks ago. So where does that leave us?"

"Gossiping like a flock of old hens, I guess," River said. "You might put your time to better use."

"True, true. I won't deny it's all just so much talk. Still, you've got to wonder about some of the people on this train. Think about it: It hadn't been two weeks since the Tal'mar airships decimated the Vangar sky-city when this train pulled out of Sanctuary. Hell, their corpses were hardly even cold."

"What's your point?"

"What was the hurry? Why were all these people in such a hurry to get out in the wilderness, when they could've stayed back in Sanctuary and had every comfort known to man?"

"I don't know... What was *your hurry*, Burk?"

Burk laughed and winked at her. "Aha! Smart girl. But I think it's time for me to get back to work now."

"Uh-huh."

Burk gathered his dishes and River watched as he handed them over to the cook's helper and went lumbering back towards the crane. She didn't take much stock in Burk's conspiracies, but River couldn't help wondering how many of the others aboard the *Iron Horse* had been entertaining the same thoughts. If it hadn't been for her conversation with Burk, it never even would have occurred to River to suspect the other crewmembers. Especially Socrates.

River finished her meal in silence, staring at the hills around the train. It didn't please her that Kale was out there somewhere, probably having the time of his life. River had volunteered to take on the duties of the train's mechanic, but she hadn't visualized it quite this way. If she'd spoken up sooner, maybe she would've ended up being the hunter, instead of Kale. Then again, hunting wasn't all that pleasant, either. There were certain disadvantages to being the hunter, especially when it was freezing cold and the entire crew was starving, and they expected you to provide something to fill their bellies.

No, River didn't want that responsibility. The truth was, she was happiest tinkering with the train's mechanical systems and helping Socrates with his projects. That was the work she found most interesting. Besides, it gave her the opportunity to work on some projects of her own without anyone prying into her business. Still, she couldn't help but feel like she was missing something. She wondered what Kale and Micah were doing out there in the darkness.

Being an automaton, Socrates didn't actually require sustenance. He'd helped serve dinner and divvy out portions of ale, but had disappeared shortly after that. When River had finished her meal, she wandered up to the crane at the front of the locomotive and found Socrates there with Burk. They had activated the *Horse's* crude electric headlamps to light the work area.

The *Iron Horse* had a few electrical conveniences, just like Sanctuary, but nothing fantastic. The engineers had already mastered steam power by the time they discovered electricity, therefore the technology had never been refined. Crude motors, generators, and electric lamps were available, but none were particularly common or effective.

River took over operating the crane and began to move the boulders while Socrates stood off to the side and directed her. Burk used his considerable strength to move the smaller rocks by hand, and used an iron pipe to leverage the larger ones to where River could better grasp them with the crane. This went on until well after midnight. Eventually, Socrates signaled for her to lower the crane.

"That's enough for today," he said. "We'll start again at first light."

"We're not half-done yet," River said. "Let's finish it!"

Socrates shook his head. "You're half-delirious with exhaustion already. I shouldn't have let you work this long."

"But a few more hours-" River started.

"-A few more hours will gain us nothing, and could cost us everything. One careless move could ruin this crane, and then where would we be? No, that risk is not acceptable. Go to your bunkrooms and rest. Replenish your strength. We will continue tomorrow."

River begrudgingly accepted his order. Technically, Socrates did have authority over the rest of the crew. It was *his* train, after all. But authority was the last reason River would follow anyone. She still wore the Vangar slave collar around her throat to remind her that those who crave authority most rarely deserve it.

Her thoughts flashed back to Lord Rutherford, the abomination of a man who had betrayed her people to the Vangars. The invaders had repaid Rutherford's loyalty by repairing his body with mechanical parts powered by steam, and then made him the ruler of the capital city. Rutherford used his power and strength to do unspeakable things to people, especially to women. His preferred type had been the small and delicate Tal'mar females, but for some reason he'd taken a special interest in River.

To this day, River had never spoken about the things Rutherford did to her. But she kept the memories fresh in her mind, and the slave collar around her throat helped her with that. River had sworn to kill any man who tried to dominate her that way again. One man on the *Horse* hadn't taken that oath seriously, until River knocked out a few of his teeth. He hadn't looked her in the eye since.

Somehow, Socrates was different. River follow-ed Socrates not because of his authority, but because of his wisdom; because of the fact that although he wasn't human, Socrates was the smartest person she'd ever met. Except for Tinker perhaps, but Tinker was long dead and his mind had been gone for some time before he finally ended his life in one desperate act to save her. If there was any creature left in the world worth following, River had decided it was Socrates. He had her undying loyalty, and that was a rare and powerful thing.

River returned to her cabin so exhausted that she fell asleep the instant she turned down the lantern. She woke to the sound of hammering. It wasn't the reverberating sound of a hammer against an anvil, but more like the steady drip of a leaking faucet, followed by a light, bell-like ringing. The sound infiltrated her dreams at first, changing things, distracting her mind, slowly luring her thoughts back to reality. After a few seconds, her eyelids fluttered open and she found herself in darkness. Judging by the path of the moon outside her window, she'd only been asleep for an hour or so.

River was tempted to roll over and go back to sleep, but curiosity got the best of her. Perhaps it was the simple fact that the crew of the *Iron Horse* was stranded in the middle of uncharted territories, and they were at the mercy of the Fates. If the train became damaged it could take weeks to repair, or if some strange creature or tribe decided to attack them, half the crew might be dead before anyone even woke.

The thought of some anonymous tribal native sneaking into her cabin to slit her throat was more than enough to get River moving. She threw back the covers and quickly pulled on her boots. She took the spring-powered revolver she had inherited from her mother from the holster hanging on her bedpost, and slipped out into the hall. She saw a light in the next car, and heard the ringing sound coming from that direction.

River stealthed her way down the walkway, across the flexible platform that separated the cars. The platform was a cleverly designed iron grating that could collapse in on itself or stretch out to several times its length. This allowed passengers to easily traverse from one car to the next while the train was in motion, even when taking corners or climbing hills. To make the journey even more convenient, many of the cars were connected by flexible canvas covers, so passengers wouldn't even have to step out into the cold.

Revolver in hand, River quietly opened the door to the next railcar and slipped inside. This was the engineering car. River was familiar with it because she had used many of the tools in the workshop. Also, one of the first things River had done after taking up residence on the *Horse* was to explore every nook and cranny of the train she could get into. That was no small task, considering that each car was the size of a small house, many were two stories tall, and the train was more than half a mile in length.

The *Horse* was so wide that it required two sets of tracks upon which to travel. Socrates had once explained that when initially designed, it was the *Iron Horse's* purpose to lay track into new territories and establish routes that would later be used by two smalller trains, one coming and the other going.

Bunk cars like the one River lived in held up to eight small apartments, some of them with multiple bunks. River, being one of the first people on board, had chosen one of the larger rooms with only one bed for herself.

She followed the noise to the workshop door and peered inside. Socrates was there, sitting on a stool at a workbench, working on some tiny piece of machinery that River didn't recognize. She stepped into the room and cleared her throat. Socrates glanced up at her and smiled apologetically.

"Ah, forgive me... did I wake you?"

Rather than tell the truth and risk hurting his feelings, River just shrugged. "What are you working on?"

Socrates climbed off the stool and made a gesture indicating she should take a look. River stepped closer to examine the tiny mechanism. What she found was a tiny metal device resting on a pedestal. It appeared to be a flat copper disk surrounded by brass rings of various sizes. She touched it with one finger, and the outer ring rotated in a gentle circle. The copper plate in the center remained in a fixed, upright position.

"What is it?" she said.

"It's an ancient technology known as a gyroscope."

"What does it do?"

"Just what you have observed," Socrates said. He tapped it, spinning all three outer rings at once. "It preserves balance, and at the same time measures angles. Imagine this mounted on a ship or a gyroplane... the pilot would know whether he was turning, climbing, or descending even if he could only see clouds around him."

"My mother could have used this," Breeze said. "But I don't understand. Why do you have it? What good is it on a train?"

"Not much, for the train itself. However, for some of us..." He winked and tapped his head. The hard metal thudded quietly under the simulated dark blue fur.

"You?" she said.

"Correct. I have one of these inside me. It helps my inner mechanisms calculate speed, direction, and balance. Without it, I would be useless."

River stared at the device with new appreciation. "I didn't realize you were so..."

"Delicate?" Socrates said with a smile. "Perhaps. But not much more so than any other creature. A human body is full of delicate, finely tuned organs. A failure of just one of them can ruin the entire system. In fact, one ancient manuscript I've read claims that humans have a tiny organ inside their ears that is filled with liquid, and performs the exact function of a gyroscope."

"Impossible," River said with a snort. "Humans don't work that way. We're not machines."

"Not exactly, but the theory is similar. As you move, the liquid in your ear moves inside this tiny organ, telling your brain what your body is doing. All of this happens automatically, without you being aware of it."

River rolled her eyes. "I've had water in my ears before, Socrates. I know *exactly* what it feels like."

Socrates grinned. "I'm sure you do... nonetheless, consider this: How many times does your heart beat in a minute? Or an hour? How many breaths do you take?"

"I don't know. I never counted them."

"And why should you? These things happen within you, mechanically. You don't need to dedicate a moment of thought to making your heart beat. Your body takes care of it for you, so you may worry about more important things."

River lifted the device, turning it over in her hands, watching that copper plate. No matter how she turned it, the plate remained upright, even when she moved it quickly.

"It's beautiful," she said, admiring the gyroscope. "It looks more like a piece of jewelry than a tool."

"Beautiful but delicate. If any of those wires twisted, or the plate bent ever so slightly, the gyroscope would fail. You may keep that one if you like. I have several more. You may want to acquaint yourself with it, if you're to learn how to maintain some of the sophisticated devices you'll encounter on this train."

"Such as?"

"All in due time," Socrates said, smiling.

Chapter 5

Micah was a light sleeper by nature. He hadn't really expected to sleep at all after the encounter they'd had earlier that evening. He was sure the haunting memories of those bizarre walking corpses would keep him up all night. Eventually though, exhaustion overwhelmed his fears and he finally managed to doze off, but his dreams were tormented -not only by images of those vile undead creatures- but also by the sound of Kale's snoring. The infernal noise woke Micah several times every hour. Each time, Micah reached out to punch Kale in the arm or pinch his nose, causing Kale to snort and roll over before falling back into a deep sleep. After a short period of silence, the snoring would resume, and Micah -just as he was drifting back to sleep- would waken abruptly and have to repeat the entire process.

At some point in the middle of the night, Micah half-woke and reached out to give his companion a shove to silence the snoring. Strangely, his hand found only empty air. Micah's dreams melted away as he touched the ground and felt warm foliage and moss next to him. Kale wasn't there. Apparently, his companion had moved to a different location.

Micah opened his eyes and blinked away the sleepiness. Through the branches overhead, he caught glimpses of bright shimmering stars and a deep midnight blue sky. A slight breeze rustled through the treetops. A few yards away, Kale's snoring rattled on, unperturbed. No, there was something wrong with that, Micah realized. The ground was still warm where Kale had been sleeping. Could Kale have moved so far away, and begun snoring again while the ground was still warm? Something about the situation didn't seem right.

That was all it took. The memory of those horrific creatures returned, and Micah immediately knew any hope for sleep was gone for the rest of the night. He slowly and cautiously pushed himself upright, his eyes boring through the darkness in the direction of the snoring. He saw a figure there, something long and flat lying across the middle of the road. The sound emanating from the creature was not snoring, he realized with considerable horror, but wheezing and grunting.

A frantic fear came over him and Micah swung his head left and right, looking for an escape. The creature in the road seemed to sense his movement. It raised its head, turning slowly to face him, and a ray of moonlight fell over the creature's face, revealing rotting flesh, exposed yellowish teeth, and empty eye sockets. A whimper escaped Micah's throat and he pushed himself back. He found himself pressed up against the stump.

Micah's noise fixated the corpse's attention. It pulled itself around and began crawling in his direction, the tattered remains of its internal organs trailing behind it like a string of sausages. This, Micah realized, must be the creature that Kale had dismembered in the crypt on the hill. Micah didn't understand how the creature could see him at first, but then he realized it was the noise he had made...

somehow, even though the creature's eyes had rotted out of its skull, it could still hear -and possibly smell- him.

Micah frantically began climbing the trunk, hoping to get out of the creature's reach. He made it halfway up before his feet slipped on the slick mossy surface and his legs went out from underneath him. As he fell, Micah struck his chin on the edge of the stump on the way down. He grunted and a shiver of terror crawled down his spine as Micah realized how much noise he'd just made. The creature was now just a few yards away and headed straight for him. Viscous green drool slathered over its chin, and guttural moaning sounds erupted forth from the corpse's throat. It clicked its rotten teeth together uncontrollably, as if it were so anxious to chew on his flesh that it was already starting without him.

Micah pushed to his feet and jumped again. The corpse lurched forward, lunging, reaching with one long decaying arm. Micah squirmed and kicked, grunting as he pulled his waistline over the edge of the stump, and the corpse's long fingernails grazed his pant leg.

As Micah pulled his legs out of reach, the creature hissed and grunted like an animal, its bony fingers and claw-like nails scratching around the base of the stump. Micah leapt to his feet. In all the excitement, he'd somehow remembered to throw his satchel over his shoulder. Thankfully, he still had it with him. He considered hurling it at the creature and almost cried out at the very thought. For Micah, the permanent loss of his precious maps and drawings was nearly equal to the horror of being eaten alive by an animated corpse. He couldn't imagine which would be worse.

Micah turned, surveying the road, calculating whether he might be able to jump over the thing and run for safety. It was then that he realized the creature was not alone. Just a few yards down the road, half a dozen more lurched and staggered towards him, their hideous faces flashing in the silvery moonlight.

Micah heard a *whooshing* sound off to his right, and spun around just in time to see the flash of a sword blade arcing through the air. It sliced effortlessly past him and through the neck of the thing crawling at his feet, instantly beheading the creature. The blade chopped into the stump like an axe as the corpse's head rolled through the grass. Kale stepped forward, placing his foot on the stump, and yanked his sword free.

"Come on," he whispered. "Crawl onto my back."

At that point, Micah was well beyond the indignity of being carried piggyback like a child. At any rate, it couldn't have been worse than being thrown over Kale's shoulder again. Kale sheathed his sword in the scabbard over his shoulder and turned his back. Micah leapt on, throwing his arms around the warrior's neck.

Kale stepped onto the road and broke into a run, holding Micah's legs to support his lightweight companion. They hadn't gone ten steps when another creature lurched out of the woods in front of them. Kale twisted frantically, reaching for his sword. Sensing the danger, Micah released his grip and dropped to the ground. He landed sideways, twisting his ankle. An involuntary yelp escaped his lips.

Kale drew his sword and Micah watched in horrified fascination as his sinewy companion raised the blade and brought it down in one swift movement, neatly decapitating the corpse. The headless body stood there, rocking back and forth, not quite realizing it was no longer whole. Kale kicked it in the chest, and the foul thing tumbled to the ground. He turned back to Micah, gesturing for his companion to follow.

Micah crawled unsteadily to his feet. Kale took off at a run and Micah hurried after him, limping as jolts of pain shot up and down his injured leg. As he passed the corpse, the awful thing reached out for his leg. Micah let out a cry and broke into a run, ignoring the pain in his ankle.

The two companions easily outdistanced their slow moving attackers, but soon both were panting with exhaustion. Micah paused to rest for a few minutes, and showed Kale his ankle.

"It's swollen alright," the warrior said grimly. "I don't think anything's broken, though. You should keep your weight off it as much as possible."

"I left my walking stick behind," Micah said.

Kale considered that. "Climb onto my back. I'll carry you."

"That's how I got hurt in the first place," Micah said, pushing awkwardly to his feet. "Help me find a crutch."

Kale hurried into the trees at the side of the road and found a suitable branch. Using his dagger, it only took a minute to shape the thing to a size appropriate for Micah's stature. Micah put the crook of the branch under his armpit and tried to walk. He made a few unsteady steps and then quickly got the hang of it.

"This will do," he said. "Let's get moving."

"Here, give me your bag. That'll make it easier to walk."

"No, I'll manage, thank you. I'd rather you kept your sword-arm free. I don't want anymore of those creatures surprising us."

After that they hurried on, neither one having any idea where they were going or when they would be able to stop. For the time, all that mattered was that they were moving, and hopefully doing so more quickly than their horrifying pursuers.

A few miles up the road, Micah pointed out distant lights in the woods off to their left.

"There!" he said. "What is that?"

"Will-o'-wisps," Kale said. "I've heard of them."

"Willow-what?"

"Wisps... fairy creatures that steal children. Never follow them into the woods at night."

"Is that so?" Micah said, pointing at the other side of the road.

There, rising out of the embankment along the trees, stood a sign. It was little more than an old rotting piece of lumber shaped like a crude arrow, with the name "Blackstone," burned across the front. It pointed to the left. Kale glanced at it and then turned, scanning the darkness ahead.

"A fork in the road," he said. "There must be a town."

"Are you sure?" Micah said sarcastically. "Perhaps it's a fairy village."

"Very funny," said Kale as he went stomping towards the fork.

The road made a few gentle turns as it meandered in the direction of the lights, and then the forest abruptly gave way to a broad clearing. They found themselves looking upon a castle. The outer wall was two stories high, and only the towers and the roof of the keep were visible beyond. The portcullis was down, barring anyone from entering or exiting the inner grounds.

"I don't see anyone up there," Kale whispered, scanning the top of the wall. "No guards or watchmen."

"Ho there!" Micah called out. "Let us in!"

Kale shot Micah a dark look, and sighed heavily.

"What?" Micah said.

"Now the whole forest knows we're here, fool."

"I hope so. I don't plan to spend the rest of the night out here with *them*."

"Are you sure? We don't even know if these people are friendly. What if the townsfolk are *them?*"

Micah gulped as he considered that. He took a few steps back and looked up and down the wall. "Maybe we could climb up and take a look," he said, his voice considerably more subdued this time.

"Not without a rope. Those stones are smooth as glass."

Kale heard a noise and spun, his hand instinctively reaching for his sword. A chill crawled down his spine as he recognized the distant lumbering shapes moving through the darkened woods up the road. It was bizarre, watching them move. The creatures were slow and plodding, but seemingly tireless. How many miles had they followed the two adventurers already? Ten, he realized, considering how many hours they'd spent traveling. Possibly closer to twelve, and yet still they came, determined as rabid bloodhounds.

"Well done," he grumbled. "You've brought the whole group down on us."

Micah raced up to the portcullis and frantically began pounding on it. "Let us in!" he cried. "Is someone there? Let us in!"

Kale, rather than being caught in the press against the wall, rushed forward to greet the oncoming mob. The nearest creature was a tall fellow that wore the unmistakable garb of a noble. Rings and jewels glittered on the creature's fingers, and a long velvet cloak adorned the monster's shoulders. In life, Kale realized, the man must have been important.

Behind the creature, more of the undead poured out of the woods. Chattering and moaning sounds erupted from their rotting chests as they zeroed in on their prey. Kale raised his sword and took a broad overhand swing at the undead noble. His sword arced down toward the creature's neck for a swift beheading, and at the same instant, Kale heard a voice cry out from behind him:

"Stop! Wait!"

Kale's sword found its mark. In one fell swoop he cleaved the noble's head clean from its neck. He turned, instinctively thrusting his blade into the belly of the nearest creature. He removed the weapon with a grunt and followed up with a powerful swing that split the creature's head in two. It dropped to the ground, and lay there, legs moving slightly as if they hadn't quite severed their connection to the brain. To make sure the job was finished, Kale took one more swing, severing the monster's neck.

"Look out!" Micah shouted behind him.

Kale saw a flicker of movement in the corner of his eye and heard footfalls accompanied by the sound of heavy breathing. He turned, brandishing his sword defensively, but found that the rest of the undead were still yards away. A lasso appeared out of the darkness and closed around his throat. Kale lashed out, trying to sever the rope, but his attacker yanked on it and pulled him off balance.

Kale turned awkwardly, staggering, struggling to hold the point of the sword high as dark shapes loomed around him. He swung wildly and his sword clanged against steel. His attackers jerked the rope again, pulling him off balance, and he stumbled. Kale dropped to one knee, and someone closed in behind and struck him solidly on the back of the head. Kale saw stars. He reached for the rope with his free hand, trying to loosen it from his neck, and swung the blade wildly in broad circles, hoping to fend off his attackers for a few more seconds. In the distance, he heard Micah cry out.

Kale raised his gaze to see his small companion being carried over a man's shoulders. They disappeared through the now partially-open portcullis. Kale jabbed the point of his broadsword into the ground in an attempt to push to his feet. As he did, a tall figure appeared next to him. Kale had a split second to take in the hawk-like features of a man with dark eyes and a week's worth of beard stubble.

Then a fist struck him solidly between the eyes and the world went dark.

Chapter 6

Micah gasped as cold water splashed across his face. He blinked and instinctively tried to throw up his arms, but found his hands were bound behind his back. He shook his head, trying to clear his vision, and saw dancing flames rising up before him.

"What is your name?"

It was a man's voice, deep and controlled. It whispered out of the darkness like velvet sliding across satin. Micah blinked, trying to see through the haze of incense and the flames. A row of urns separated him from some sort of tall, bizarre-looking machinery at the front of the room. The machine appeared to be mostly made of iron, but he caught glimpses of brass gears and copper pipes weaving in and out along the framework. He twisted, struggling against the bonds that held him in his chair, and the tip of a sword appeared and pressed to his throat.

"Don't make me repeat myself," the voice said.

"Micah. My name is Micah. I'm from a village in the west."

"And who brought you here?"

"I came alone!"

"Liar!" someone shouted behind him. The sword point pressed closer, biting into his flesh. Micah grimaced.

"Stay your hand," the voice said. "There is no benefit in destroying this tiny creature. Bring the wine."

"Yes, Keeper."

The sword blade vanished. Micah heard footsteps moving in the darkness behind him. Ahead, beyond the flames, a shadow separated from the curtains that surrounded the machine. A man appeared. He was tall and thin with a long beard, clothed in dark robes with a hood pulled over his head that concealed most of his face.

"You will find we are not unforgiving," the stranger said in a hypnotic monotone. A goblet appeared before Micah and the guard pressed it to his lips.

"Drink," a second guard nearby commanded.

Micah considered resisting, and quickly decided against it. The thought of that sword pressed against his throat was enough to convince him not to fight. If the wine was poisoned, at least it would be over quickly rather than the hours of torture the guards would probably subject him to.

Micah gulped the wine. It spilt over his chin, forming into rivulets that streamed down his throat and trickled across the bare, pale skin of his chest. The liquid was warm and bitter on the tongue with an acidic bite; a poorly made wine from poorly grown grapes. The slightly sweet aftertaste was herbaceous and grassy, like a mouthful of leaves, and Micah wondered if that was the flavor of the poison or if someone had simply sweetened the wine to make it palatable.

At last, the goblet disappeared. Micah gulped down the last swallow and closed his eyes, focusing on the warm sensation that spread through his limbs. A drop of water fell from his bangs and ran down his nose. The fire in the urns before him crackled. Micah noticed a numb tingling sensation in his lips, and suddenly began to feel very relaxed.

"Let's start from the beginning," the robed stranger said. "What is your name?"

"Erm.. ma name is... Miyyyyykah."

"Did you come here alone, Micah?"

In his mind's eye, Micah saw Kale. The large man wore a look of absolute horror on his face as he raced out of the cemetery gate screaming, "Run! Run for your life!" The image ran so counter to everything that Micah knew about Kale that he couldn't help laughing. Kale, the tall, cocky warrior - the man with a chest like a barrel and arms like tree trunks- running away in absolute terror. It was just about the funniest thing Micah had ever seen. He threw his head back and the sound of his full-throated laughter came erupting out uncontrollably, echoing back and forth in the darkness around him.

Chapter 7

Kale woke to a deep throbbing pain in his skull. He moaned, reaching for his forehead, and heard more than felt the chains that bound his wrists. His eyes fluttered open and at first, he saw only a single ray of light beaming down through a crack in the exposed timber ceiling high above. Gradually, the iron bars of his cell came into focus. The mildewed scent of rotting straw and human waste filled his nostrils. Kale rolled over to vomit on the floor. It didn't take long to empty the contents of his stomach. He moaned, spitting the taste of bile from his mouth, wiping the dribble away on the back of his sleeve.

"Very poetic," said a man's voice. "I guess I won't be sleeping there anymore."

Kale backed away from the mess and pushed to his knees. The world spun, twisting drunkenly around him. He saw the vague outline of a man leaning against the far wall, but couldn't separate the body from the shadows. Awkwardly, he rose to his feet.

"Sorry," he said, kicking straw over the mess he'd left on the floor. Rays of sunshine streamed in through the narrow window at the end of the room, illumining the floor in a tall rectangle of light. Through the opening, Kale saw a few scattered rooftops, and a deep blue sky painted with snow-white clouds. Slowly, somewhat painfully, his vision at last came into focus.

Kale twisted his head, taking in his surroundings. He was in a cage of iron that was bolted to a stone floor. Half a dozen similar cages surrounded him, scattered throughout the room, along with miscellaneous ancient torture devices. Halfway across the room, he saw the dark silhouetted shape of another prisoner watching them. In an adjacent cell, he noticed a small body lying on the floor and realized that it could only be Micah. His companion appeared to be sleeping.

"Where am I?" Kale said.

The man in the corner stepped forward, and a beam of light fell across his face. He was a good-looking fellow with fine, almost stately features. His jaw was strong but lean, like his build; both too feminine to be called rugged or anything like it. He had bright green mischievous eyes. He smiled and reached out for Kale's hand, and Kale noted that the man's teeth were perfectly straight and unusually white. He decided instantly that the man was in fact a noble.

"You are in the northern tower of Blackstone Castle," the man said, shaking his hand. "Once the barracks, but now a jail for prisoners like us. There are only two ways out of here: The first is through that door, which is guarded night and day. The second is the window. There's a narrow ledge that leads to the battlements and into the keep, but make one false step and you'll drop a hundred feet to the courtyard. In case you were wondering, that is."

"Who are you? How do you know all of this?"

"I've been here nearly a month. I almost escaped once, when I first arrived. I overpowered a guard and took his key to unlock my cell. I went to the window to test the escape route and found it impossible. For a full-grown man, at any rate. As for your first question, I am Thane, poet and bard of the royal court at Avenston."

"Avenston?" Kale echoed. "You're from Astatia?"

"Where else?"

Kale looked him up and down, noting Thane's fine leathers and worn but clearly expensive clothes. Thane's vest was dark green leather, no doubt intended to set off his bright eyes. His shirt was made of fine white silk and his breeches were black suede. He also wore a black velvet cloak and knee-high boots, and topped off the look with a distinguished stovepipe hat.

Kale's gaze fell on the silver pendant around the man's neck. It was shaped like an ancient oak, the symbol of an aristocrat or other public figure in Avenston. Despite the stains of travel and hard use, there was no doubt in Kale's mind that Thane was telling the truth. He was indeed a bard.

"You're a long way from home," Kale said. "I lived in Avenston once, while the Vangars still ruled."

"What do you mean?" Thane said, raising his eyebrows. "The Vangars have fallen?"

"You didn't know?" Kale said. "The Tal'mar discovered Sanctuary, the city of the ancients. They attacked the Vangars with a fleet of airships and overthrew them in a single night. They forced the Vangars into slavery to repay their debts!"

"I never dreamed of such a thing!" Thane said. "Such tidings... Shayla and I thought we'd never be able to return-" Thane leapt forward threw his arms around the burly warrior. "Thank you Kale, for this wonderful news!"

"Who is Shayla?" Kale said, somewhat uncomfortably trying to extricate himself from the bard's arms. Thane stepped away, grinning broadly. "Shayla is my companion... she's over there." He pointed in the direction of the far cell. The silhouette moved, suddenly revealing the decidedly feminine features of a woman with long hair and a slender build.

"Well met, stranger," she said with a wave. "Wonderful news indeed, were we not all locked up in a cell and awaiting execution."

Kale's gazed danced back and forth between the two of them. "Execution?" he said. "They mean to kill us?"

"Not yet," said Thane. "First you'll have a hearing. The execution doesn't come until the full moon. That's what we've been waiting for. We have a day or two..."

"But I don't understand... why would they want to kill us?"

"As a punishment," Thane said.

"For what? I haven't done anything! I only wanted into the castle to escape those..." his eyes flashed as he searched for a word to describe the creatures that remained so vividly in his memory.

"Those monsters?" Thane said. "That, my friend, is your crime: Murder!"

Kale searched the bard's face in disbelief. "Murder? But those... *things* are already dead."

"So it would seem," said Thane. "Nonetheless, these backwoods peasants don't take kindly to their relatives being killed... even the ones who are —as you say- already dead."

"You can't be serious."

"Indeed, I am. You've stumbled into a castle of nightmares, my friend. Our only consolation lies in the fact that it will all be over soon. When the moon is full, two days hence, our captors will *burn us alive.*"

Kale's mind flashed back to the *Iron Horse* and he suddenly, fervently hoped Socrates had finished the work of clearing the tracks and that they were now looking for him. The rational part of his mind told him they probably hadn't even realized he was missing yet. His gaze strayed to his unconscious companion.

"Micah!" Kale called out. "Micah, wake up!"

The shape on the floor stirred. Micah slowly roused himself. He grumbled as he crawled to his feet and turned to face Kale. He grabbed the bars with both hands, pressing his face against them.

"So cool..." he said absently, touching his forehead to the bars.

"Micah, we've been captured!"

Micah nodded slightly and waved off Kale's concern. He closed his eyes for a moment and then opened them again, staring across the room. "They took my maps, Kale. My satchel, my parchments, my ink... what will I do?"

"I'd say that's the least of our problems right now. They plan to execute us."

Micah's eyes widened. "No, they can't! Then I'll never get my maps back!"

"That's one way to put it," said Thane with a wry grin. He turned his attention to Kale. "Your small friend came in a few hours after they dumped you in here. He appeared to be drugged. My guess is they spent that time questioning him."

"Is that true, Micah?"

The impish man scratched the back of his head. "Aye, I think so. I don't remember much."

Kale stepped up to the bars and gave Micah a dark look. "What did you tell them? Think about it! Did you mention the *Horse?*"

Micah frowned. He pinched his chin and paced back and forth along the front of his cage. "I don't remember... I honestly don't remember."

"Don't blame him," Thane said. "They've done the same thing to Shayla and me. Neither of us could remember a thing... What is this 'horse' you speak of?"

Kale looked Thane up and down, wondering if he could trust the man. It was one thing to share stories of their old kingdom, but quite another to hand over vital information that an enemy might use against them. The couple seemed trustworthy enough, but for all Kale new, Thane and Shayla might have been informants working with the townsfolk.

"It's nothing," he said. "Nothing important."

"Ah, I see," said Thane. "It sounded like something important. No matter. Tell me, have you ever been to the *Dancing Dragon Inn* on Merchant Row?"

"Oh, please!" Shayla shouted across the room. "Not this again. So you played for a duchess. No one cares, Thane."

"I just thought he might know of her," Thane said dejectedly. "Not that it matters. Titles of nobility meant nothing after the Vangars invaded. Still, she was a model among women. I can still remember her sweet lips..." He leaned back against the cage and bent over slightly, lifting the heel of his boot. He touched an invisible pressure point on the side of his boot and a small door opened on the back of the heel. Thane grinned as he withdrew a short straight razor and a tiny mirror.

"If she truly is a duchess, she's lucky to be alive at all," said Kale, eyeing the bard as he wetted the razor in a cup of water and started to shave. Kale stepped over to the door of the cell and began fumbling with the lock. "No offense, but I think we'd be better off using our time to find a way out of here before they execute us, don't you?"

"Yes!" Micah agreed from his cage.

"Unlikely," said Thane. "You won't open those locks without a key. We've already tried everything else. These iron bars are unbreakable, and the stones in the floor are immovable. It would take years to chisel through either, and we don't have a chisel. We have nothing but our clothes and the straw under our feet. The watchmen saw to that before they threw us in here."

"Have you tried this?" said Micah. With surprising dexterity, he latched onto the bars and began climbing towards the roof of his cage.

"I take it your ankle feels better," Kale said.

"Much," said Micah, grunting as he heaved himself up towards the ceiling.

"What are you doing up there, little one?" Shayla called out. "That cage has bars on the ceiling, too."

"They're not as narrow up there," Micah grunted as he pulled himself up. He reached the top of the wall and then twisted around to stand with his heels perched on a crossbar, somewhat awkwardly facing the inside of his cage.

"Careful," said Thane. "A fall from that height might break your legs, or worse, your neck."

Kale sized up the distance and realized Thane was right. The roof of the cage was ten, maybe twelve feet high. A survivable drop for a human, but for a man Micah's size it may as well have been twice that.

"What are you doing?" Kale shouted. "Get down from there before you break that ankle for real."

Micah ignored his companion. He took a moment to summon up his courage and then leapt. Kale caught his breath as Micah flew to the center of the cage and latched onto the bars along the roof with both hands. An involuntary squeal erupted out of Shayla. Micah hung suspended in midair, swaying back and forth more than ten feet over the stone floor.

"Devils, Micah," Kale shouted. "Think about what you're doing!"

"Quiet!" Micah commanded breathlessly. He began to pull himself upwards, twisting back and forth as he tried to work his way through the bars. His short legs kicked wildly in the air as he struggled. To Kale's surprise, a moment later Micah's head appeared on the outside of the cage.

"He's getting tired," Thane observed quietly. "I hope his strength holds out. It won't be pretty if your friend gets stuck up there with his head between the bars."

Kale grimaced at the thought of watching Micah accidentally hang himself. "Keep going!" he said supportively. "Push yourself up!" He couldn't entirely banish the nervousness from his voice. Micah flailed around for a few more seconds and then managed to get his arms through the bars. He moved upward, but couldn't slide his chest through the tight space.

"Thanks," Micah said cynically, fighting for breath. "Great idea, Kale. Really, very useful."

Kale frowned. "Just trying to be helpful," he murmured.

Micah rolled his eyes, twisting as he struggled to push his upper body between the bars, legs still kicking wildly in the air. "It appears..." he said breathlessly, "that I'm *stuck*."

"Exhale," Thane said helpfully. "Let your air out!"

Micah grunted. For a few seconds, he stopped moving. Then, he let his breath out in one great *whoosh,* and pushed. For a moment, it seemed to work. He made it halfway through the bars and then something caught, and held him in place. Micah twisted, grunting, struggling wildly. He tried to take a small breath, but found even that impossible. He was trapped with his chest centered between the bars so tightly that he couldn't even breathe! Spots swam before his eyes and darkness closed in at the edges of his vision.

"Try again!" Kale said encouragingly. "Push, Micah!"

"Yes," Shayla shouted. "Keep going. Don't stop pushing!"

Micah had heard this sort of thing before. An image of a birthing room sprouted up in the back of his mind, and he visualized himself as a tiny infant pushing through a narrow birth canal of steel bars. The ludicrous image almost made him laugh as it floated through his addled mind, except that Micah couldn't laugh. Already, he felt consciousness slipping away, his thoughts drifting dizzily into darkness.

This was it, he realized. This was how he was going to die. This cage giving birth to him was going to kill him. Died in childbirth. No, not childbirth, manbirth. He'd already been born once. How many people got to be born twice? What a story that would make for the taverns! Born into the world, born into death. That was what they'd put on his epitaph. Then they'd all have a good laugh. If there was one thing Micah was always good for, it was a laugh.

Micah's energy was ebbing. The world grew distant, and the sound of blood roaring through his veins filled his ears. This, he realized, was death. This was what it was like to die.

Deep inside his chest, something fluttered, and a surge of terror washed through him. The spark of life that was Micah suddenly announced that it didn't want to die. In a surge of adrenaline-fueled panic, Micah summoned his strength and gave one last desperate push. The bars pinched his ribcage like the grips of a vise, squeezing out one tiny last bit of breath. Micah heard the distant, muffled sound of tearing fabric, and without realizing what it was, felt the release of a button ripping free of his jacket. Instantly, the bars lost their grip on him. Micah shot up through the opening. He came to rest on top of the cage with his legs dangling down.

Micah sucked in a deep gasping breath and lay back across the bars, waiting for the world to stop spinning. In the background, he could hear his companions cheering quietly. His thoughts spun dizzily. For a moment, he may have even passed out. As the world slowly came back into perspective, all Micah could think about was how close he'd come to a horrible -and somewhat embarrassing- death. The word *stillborn* rolled around in his mind, and a surge of nausea almost made him vomit.

When at last Micah felt half normal again, he pushed up into a seated position and glanced down at his vest. "Blast it!" he said angrily. He threw his gaze down to the floor and saw the button lying there in the middle of the cell. "I'll never find a replacement for that button!"

"Button?" Kale said loudly. "Forget the button, Micah. Get us out of here!"

Micah lifted his gaze to his companions and at last remembered the point of his expedition. "How?" he said. "I can't open the locks."

"Not without keys," Thane reminded him. "The guards keep them outside. I already told you, we're trapped."

"I think I can get out," Micah said, eyeing the window on the far wall. "I'll go for help."

"No, wait!" Kale said. "Don't leave us in here."

Micah crawled down the outside of his cage and nonchalantly walked over to the window, carefully

71

keeping the weight off his still tender ankle. The window was out of reach, but after a quick search he turned up a chair that would suffice.

Kale continued to protest as Micah clambered up onto the chair and pulled himself up over the window ledge. Micah ignored him. There was no time to reason with Kale, nor to explain that the more time they wasted arguing, the less likely it was that he'd actually get away in time to get help. Wordlessly, Micah slipped through the window and vanished. As he climbed out onto the ledge, he heard Kale mutter the words, "Now he's gonna get himself killed for sure."

We'll see about that, Micah thought defiantly. He'd already had one brush with death. There had to be some rule about that. Then he glanced down and realized that he was standing on a six-inch ledge, staring down at a hundred foot drop to the paving stones.

Chapter 8

When River woke the next morning, the sky was clear, the weather was reasonably warm, and Kale and Micah were nowhere to be found. River didn't think much of their absence, except to take some little satisfaction in the fact that she knew Kale better than he knew himself. As she'd told Burk, her irresponsible friend was probably sleeping out on the prairie somewhere, and more than likely lost. She didn't give the matter a second thought. She went back to work restoring the tracks, and the hours began ticking away.

When Kale still hadn't arrived by midmorning, River simply rolled her eyes and imagined him snoring away under a rock or bush somewhere. She felt a little sympathy for Micah, being stuck with the obstinate warrior, but that had been his decision.

Then, when they had finished clearing the tracks and the crew began gathering for lunch, River at last began to worry. She went to Socrates with her concerns.

"We have a few hours of work yet," he reminded her. "One of the tracks has been damaged and we'll have to replace it. Perhaps they will return before we finish."

"It's not like Kale to be gone this long," River said.

"It's not?"

"Well, it is... I mean, I understand him not showing up last night and even oversleeping this morning. But Kale should have known we'd be finished by now. He would have come back."

"I'm not sure I agree with your assessment," Socrates said, "but you have known Kale much longer than I have and you may be right. Unfortunately, we can't organize a search party with so much work left. The crane must be dismantled, and the tracks repaired. Perhaps when we are done..."

"Forget a search party," River said. "I'll go look for them. You don't need me to finish the tracks, and any fool could dismantle the crane. Let *me* go."

Socrates considered that. "And if they *did* find trouble?" he said. "Should I send one person out, when two couldn't manage to come back? No, I'd prefer you wait. We don't need to lose a third crew member."

River relented. She took her food to an empty table and ate in silence, trying not to think about her frustration. Instead, she ended up eavesdropping on a conversation between Burk and one of the other crewmates. His companion was human, apparently from South Bronwyr, judging by the man's provincial drawl. He was middle-aged with a bald head and clean-shaven, round face. He wore an eye patch on his right eye and the rest of the crew called him - appropriately- Patch.

"I don't believe it," Burk said. "Socrates can't be human. He's got a smokestack on his head fer Lordan's sake."

"I didn't say he was *human*," Patch replied. "I said 'e' was jus' like a human. Thinkin' and everythin'."

"Aye, he thinks right enough, but does he feel? Of course not!"

"I'm nae sure," said Patch. "I've seen him talkin' to the others and I'm right certain 'e's more than just gears and gizmos. He may 'ave started as a machine, but he ain't one now. Somethin' happened, makin' 'im think and feel, just like us."

The burly blacksmith dismissed his baldheaded companion with a snort. "You're projecting," he muttered. He took a big bite of roast and the greasy juices streamed down his beard. He appeared not to notice.

"Aye, like you know what that means," Patch said, rolling his eyes. "Don' be slingin' those silvery words 'round here."

"It means ya see in him what ain't there; what yer seein' is yerself."

"Pfft," was Patch's educated response.

That was the end of the argument, and River didn't stick around long enough to hear the next one. She finished her meal and went back to work. She started by driving the steamwagon back to the storage car, and then recruited two other crewmembers to help disassemble the crane. For the next few hours, she threw herself into her work.

Later, as the afternoon wore on, her thoughts returned to her childhood friend and for the first time, she began to doubt Socrates' judgment. The conversation between Burk and his companion had planted a seed in the back of her mind, a lingering doubt that she couldn't quite ignore, and River found herself wondering if those two fools had accidentally hit on something important. In their own illiterate way, Burk and Patch had stumbled onto a question that River realized she didn't have an obvious answer to. Just how *human* was Socrates? He could think and reason, but could he *feel?* That seemed important.

River had just returned one of the long iron trusses to its place in the cargo car. She stood in the doorway a moment, staring out over the hills, feeling the cold wind splash across her skin and began to realize she was worried. That wasn't an entirely new sensation when it came to Kale. Though he was a decade older than River, he usually behaved more like a child than a man, and she often found herself thinking of him like a younger brother. When River felt that stirring of concern inside her, she realized for the first time that for all his wisdom and knowledge, Socrates was *not* human. He was a machine. And how could she trust a machine to make life and death decisions if it couldn't even *feel?*

It didn't take much of that thinking to convince River that Burk had been right all along. Socrates may have been smart, but he lacked the all-important emotions that would have tempered his judgment. Therefore, his decision to continue working must have been based purely on logic. It was the decision of a machine, not of a caring and sympathetic human being.

Once that was decided, it was only a matter of waiting for the right opportunity. The moment the others weren't looking, River slipped away to her quarters to retrieve her spring-powered revolver. She quickly strapped the holster to her waist and then went racing down the hall towards a very special boxcar halfway down the train. Inside, River had found a collection of steam engines and other miscellaneous parts during her explorations of the *Iron Horse*. In secret, River had been using some of those parts to build a special project of her own. No one knew of it, not even Kale, and probably not even Socrates.

River quietly slipped inside the boxcar. There, she pulled the canvas tarp off of her project and released it from the safety straps. River's two-wheeled *boneshaker* wasn't exactly like the one Tinker had made, but it was close. Instead of an oil-burning gyroplane engine, this one had a small but powerful steam engine. It also had a wider, more stable stance and a spring-cushioned leather seat to reduce some of the bone-shaking that had inspired the invention's name. River checked the water level in the holding tank and then fired up the burner. As the flames licked up against the bottom of the tank, the brass pressure gauge came to life. Within minutes, the *boneshaker* was ready to go.

"Burk, secure that rail," Socrates said as several crewmen maneuvered the heavy iron track into place. Burk's assistant held a spike in place as the smith brought his mallet down with enough force to crush the man's hand. One blow drove the steel shaft halfway into the wooden tie. The second drove it home.

"Good," Socrates said. "The rest of you, secure the other ties. Burk and I will fetch another rail."

Socrates heard a deep-throated rumbling sound in the distance. He turned to stare down the line. Nearly half a mile in the distance, close to the far end of the *Iron Horse*, the boneshaker roared to life and came flying out of a boxcar. As it touched down at the bottom of the embankment and roared up the opposite hill leaving a cloud of dust in its wake, Socrates recognized River sitting astride the vehicle.

"What was that?" someone said.

Socrates fixed his jaw and glared at the cloud of dust floating over the hill. "I knew she'd eventually do something like that," he mumbled as the dust dissipated on the breeze. The sound of the motorcycle rumbled in the distance.

"What should we do?" one of the workers said.

"Nothing. Get back to work."

River couldn't help but feel a twinge of guilt as she vanished over the hill. After all, she considered Socrates her friend. He was an extraordinary machine and almost human, in his way. River's admiration wasn't enough to make her turn back, though. When she felt his eyes boring into her back, she ignored the guilt gnawing at her insides and focused her eyes on the horizon.

River's conflicted emotions aside, the sense of elation that washed over her as she felt the boneshaker between her legs and the icy wind whipping at her hair made her forget everything else. It had been a long time since she'd ridden. Too long. River twisted the throttle and surged forward, flying over the rolling terrain with surprising ease. So far, the coil springs she'd added to the seat's suspension system were working wonderfully.

River hadn't worn any goggles. She blinked her watering eyes and eased back on the throttle. If she'd learned anything from the previous boneshaker, it was that at high speed, bugs hurt. Devils, if one struck her in the eye it might blind her. She let the speed burn off and then idled to a stop on top of a hill about a mile north of the *Horse*. It was a high vantage point, and she saw the forest rising in the east. In every other direction, she saw only rolling hills and wild grain.

Kale had supposedly gone hunting, but River saw no signs of wildlife. He'd probably gone straight for the woods. She revved up the throttle and took off, aiming for the plateau to the northeast. Just like her companions, River thought it would make an excellent spot to scout out the lay of the land.

River managed her speed carefully, keeping an eye out for dangerous rocks and holes in the ground that might damage the boneshaker. Even so, she made the journey in a fraction of the time it had taken her companions. She reached the graveyard in twenty minutes, and parked outside the gate. She sat there a moment, steam vapors rising up around her from the boneshaker's exhaust, stared at the eerie mass of decaying tombs and gravestones.

There was something disquieting about the cemetery; something not just out of place but *wrong*. River's skin crawled with the feeling that she was being watched. She turned slowly, searching the ruins for any sign of her companions. She noted nothing until she turned back to the east and saw, lying at the edge of the hill, a small shape glinting in the sunlight. River lowered the kickstand, dismounted the boneshaker, and hurried over to the mysterious object. She snatched it up and examined it. To her surprise, River realized it was a small inkwell.

Her senses alert, River slowly drew her gaze across the hillside and noted the bizarre tracks mingling in the dusty earth. She isolated Micah's prints easily enough, and the large boot prints must have belonged to Kale, but what about the others? River frowned as she noticed the strange markings of legs twisted sideways or dragged behind. Some of the prints revealed open heels or toes, as if the owners of the shoes had worn them completely raw and continued on with parts of their feet sticking out.

A few yards away, River found the most horrifying tracks of all. She found the trail of a creature with the hands of a man, but crawling on its belly. Along the trail, she found scattered pieces of torn flesh and entrails, as if someone had dragged the corpse of an animal down the hill. This was no animal, though, it was a man, and judging by the handprints along the trail, he was moving under his own power.

River stifled a chill as she climbed back onto the boneshaker and, somewhat hesitantly, began her descent into those murky woods.

Chapter 9

Micah wasn't one to complain. Despite his pounding headache and the periodic waves of nausea, he had accepted his lot and taken up the task of saving his companions -not just Kale, but the other two as well. Micah didn't know anything about the other prisoners, except that they had been there when he woke, and that they would probably share the same unfortunate fate if they weren't rescued. That was why he planned on going straight to Socrates.

Micah knew better than trying to rescue the others alone. He couldn't get them out of the tower without being seen, and he certainly couldn't fight off the guards himself. This was a complicated situation, and complicated situations called for complicated leaders. Micah couldn't think of anyone in the world more complicated than the mechanical gorilla who commanded the crew of the *Horse*. Socrates would know what to do.

This was what he told himself as he slipped quietly through the battlements, leaping from one shadow to the next. Micah stopped to lean around a tall stone parapet. He glanced down into the courtyard, where countless townsfolk came and went through the town square, and several dozen maids - old and young alike- had gathered to wash clothes and trade gossip. So far everything was quiet. No one had raised the alarm yet, and so far no one had seen him. In another hundred yards or so, he'd make it to the overhanging trees and he'd be home free.

Micah turned his gaze back towards the tower behind him. He couldn't help but worry -not so much about his companion, but about his maps. The guards had taken Micah's satchel when they brought him to the tower, and on the way inside they had tossed it aside like a worthless bag of horse manure. It pained him deeply to think of the way they had discarded it, more still to imagine it lying there in the mud next to the stables. Micah's drawings were his most precious possessions. They were his heart and soul, and it would devastate him should they be destroyed.

Unfortunately, the stables and his satchel were in the wrong direction, around the far side of the tower and well out of sight. The only way to save them would be to go back for them, and as much as it pained him, Micah knew that wouldn't be right. He couldn't risk getting caught again. No, he had to get out of the castle, find the rail tracks again, and race back to the *Iron Horse* to find Socrates.

Micah pushed aside the thoughts of his drawings (as much as he could) and hurried the rest of the way to the trees, where they were hanging over the edge of the outer wall. He finally felt safe as he alighted onto a narrow branch and pushed through the foliage towards the trunk. This was a familiar environment for Micah, the sheltered safety of the treetops. In the village of his youth, many of the homes were built in the trees for protection from wild animals and marauding trolls. Micah was comfortable there, so much so that he was tempted to stay there a while, until things calmed down.

Unfortunately, that wasn't an option. Time was of the essence, and for the sake of his paintings as well as his friend, Micah had to keep moving. He hurried towards the trunk and from there, quickly scrambled down the branches to the mossy ground. He landed with a quiet *thump* and paused, scanning the woods around him.

A bird chirped in a nearby nest, and a wild hare vanished into the undergrowth to the east. He heard the distant murmuring voices; the sounds of people talking inside the castle wall. Other than that, he seemed to be alone. Still, Micah patiently waited. He knew that if something lurked in those woods, it would eventually move. He wasn't about to go carelessly running about and land in the arms of one of those *creatures* again.

After some time, Micah had observed nothing more than a stirring of the wind in the branches overhead and a few blue jays harassing a lone raven. He finally decided that no one had followed him, and that none of those undead corpses were lurking in the surrounding wilderness. He leapt to his feet and went racing through the trees.

Micah tore through the underbrush as fast as his legs could carry him, leaping fallen logs and zigzagging between the trees. Shortly, the woods thinned out and gave way to a narrow stretch of the same river that they had crossed the previous night. The bridge was nowhere in sight. If his memory of the landscape was correct, it lay a mile or more to the south. That seemed a long distance to travel, when he could just as easily cross the river here.

That water was relatively deep, but the current was slow and a series of boulders formed what almost seemed to be a path across the river. Micah decided that backtracking to the bridge would be foolish. It would take too long, and it would vastly increase his chances of running into more guards or more of those walking undead.

"No, this will have to do," he said quietly, stepping down the embankment. He maneuvered himself close to the water's edge and then stepped easily onto the first large rock at the edge of the riverbank. He took a moment to gauge the best crossing and then began leaping deftly from one stone to the next.

Micah had strength and agility that would have surprised most of his crewmates, though he did pay extra attention to the ankle he had twisted the day before. It seemed to have recovered nicely, but he didn't dare put any extra pressure on it. If his ankle gave out on him now, in the middle of nowhere and miles away from the train, he'd be in some real trouble.

Micah easily made it from the first stone to the next, and then across two more before he finally came to a standstill. Halfway across the river Micah paused, perched on top of a boulder, and turned his head slowly, searching for his next landing. He was still half a dozen yards from the opposite bank and there was a large stretch of empty space between this boulder and the next. However, upon closer inspection, Micah realized that just two yards away was another boulder hiding just beneath the surface of the water. He could see the jagged, shiny top peaking up from the murky waters.

Micah was willing to make the jump and risk getting his feet wet, but unfortunately, the boulder was just out of reach. Micah was an excellent jumper, but doubted seriously that he could jump that far under those conditions. And he really wasn't a very good swimmer, either. The village of his youth had been high on a mountain, far from the streams and lakes where another child might have learned to swim. He'd seen a boat once; a long birch bark canoe operated by several trolls in a river on the plains, but hadn't thought about it much at the time. He'd been more worried about trying to stay out of sight. Now he wished he had one. A boat that was, not a troll.

Micah stooped over slightly, trying to catch a glimpse of what else might lie beneath the surface. One more good-sized stone between the two, and he'd be home free. He saw his image reflected back at him in the choppy surface, and the canopy of trees overhead. He saw the deep blue sky and puffy white clouds drifting slowly across the heavens, mirrored in the movement of the water. Then, just a few feet away, he saw a reflection. Was it a stone? He couldn't be sure.

Micah knelt closer, dropping to his knees as he struggled to separate the images reflected on the surface from the submerged objects lurking below. He craned his head to the side. When that failed, he reached out and splashed his hand across the surface in an attempt to break up the reflections; to verify that the stone was actually there and not just an artifact of light and shadow. Perched that way on the edge of the boulder with his arm stretched so far that he was about to topple, Micah had all but guaranteed himself a good soaking.

With a sudden spray of water, something broke the surface and latched onto his wrist. A horrified squeal erupted from Micah's throat as he tumbled head over heels and crashed into the water. For a moment, panic swept over him and he could do nothing but thrash violently as he sank into the icy darkness. Micah recognized the grip of the undead creature and it put a greater fear into him than anything he had ever known. He felt the rotting flesh and cold, unyielding bone against his skin. In a frenzied panic, he thrashed and kicked at the unseen enemy, struggled against it for all he was worth.

Somehow, Micah broke loose of the creature's grip. Caught up in the current, he bounced and rolled along the stones at the river bottom, hammering into the submerged boulders as the river's momentum carried him downstream. The sky flashed through his vision, tinted green from the murky water, and hazy rays of light streamed down from above like bands of sunshine frozen in time. Rocks slammed into him, driving the breath from his lungs, and spots swam before his eyes.

The current swept him sideways, and the eddies carried Micah towards the bank. He slammed into an underwater log and the force of the impact drove the last bubbles of oxygen from his lungs. Micah knew he had only seconds before his body's natural instincts took over. He clenched his teeth as spasms shook his chest and the muscles in his abdomen contracted, forcing him to inhale. Micah couldn't fight it any longer. He had to breathe...

Then, miraculously, he felt the gravelly river bottom under his feet. Micah kicked at the ground and simultaneously pushed away from the log. He broke through the surface with a splash, wheezing and gasping for air, coughing as the water gagged him. He spit the liquid out and sucked in huge gasping breaths of air. Micah wasn't much of a swimmer, but his instincts took over and kept him afloat. He kicked his legs and paddled his arms, and somehow managing to remain buoyant long enough to catch his breath.

When at last the ache in his lungs diminished and his senses began to return, Micah turned slowly, treading water as the gentle movement carried him further downstream. All around him, Micah saw the trees and the sky reflected in the choppy surface of the water. Horrifying visions danced through his head of what lurked under the surface. He'd seen the creature. He knew it was down there somewhere. Perhaps there were more!

Frantically, he began paddling toward the shore.

*

River heard Micah's cries over the roar of the boneshaker's engine and the rush of wind in her ears. At first, she thought she'd heard a young girl screaming.

River braked the boneshaker and pulled the pressure lever, letting the excess steam vapors out of the tank. It gave off a momentary hiss and then went silent. She sat there for a moment astride the powerful machine, her senses straining for some indication of what she'd heard. Birds chirped in the branches overhead and swooped through the sky, observing some ancient instinctive mating ritual. The trees swayed, moaning, gusts of wind shaking the tree tops. All around her, River observed the signs of life and vibrancy one might expect in an unspoiled forest. And yet nothing else. Not a sound or movement to indicate what she had heard.

River decided it must have been her imagination and reached for the pressure valve. With her hand on the lever, she stopped. A painful-sounding gasp came from the woods off to her left. River's hand went instinctively to her revolver as she scanned the woods along the embankment. The terrain was too dense for the boneshaker to navigate, so River parked the vehicle and hurried towards the sound on foot. Branches slapped at her face and scratched her arms as she plunged into the forest, her revolver still drawn and ready.

River forced her way through the branches and leapt out onto the embankment. Micah was just a few yards away, climbing the riverbank. Panicked cries emanated out of him, though he didn't even seem aware of the sounds he was making. He scrambled and splashed up the muddy bank like a man gone insane, driven only by some deep primal fear of whatever lay behind him.

"Micah!" River yelled as she hurried in his direction. "What happened? Where's Kale?"

Micah flinched at the sound of her voice. Then, realizing who it was, he scurried along the bank towards her at full tilt. River reached out to help him climb the edge of the embankment. She caught his hand and pulled him up, lifting the diminutive man off his feet. She set him on dry ground and Micah stood before her shaking, white as a sheet, eyes wide with terror.

"Go," he muttered incoherently as he pushed past her. "Must go. Must go!"

River frowned as she turned to watch Micah race into the woods behind her. She pulled her gaze away from the small man and looked back towards the river. At that very moment, one of the hideous undead corpses came crawling out of the water with a loud splash. The bizarre, mutilated creature latched onto a boulder along the riverbank and drew itself awkwardly upright. It turned slowly, as if listening intently, and then fixed its gaze on her. River's blood froze as she saw the thing's grinning deathmask of a face. Its eyes were empty sockets, and the flesh had rotted away, revealing more skull than skin. She lifted her gaze and saw several more along the opposite bank, slowly wading into the water.

Without thinking, River raised her arm and fired the revolver. The spring action made little more than a clicking sound as she squeezed the trigger, but the explosive eruption of the bullet's shockwave was almost as loud as a small musket. Her aim was true, and the projectile slammed into the creature's forehead. The monster's skull cracked open and a trickle of blood issued forth. The undead thing staggered and dropped onto its back, twitching.

Just behind it, three more came crawling out of the water. River moved her arm to realign the sights, but then realized the creature she had just shot was moving again. It flopped awkwardly like a beached

89

fish as it struggled to regain its footing. Slowly but surely, the creature rolled onto its belly and crawled back to its knees. Within seconds it was back on its feet, ambling towards her. River turned back to see Micah lurking a few yards back. At last, she fully understood the source of his terror.

"Now?" he said in a half-whisper.

River nodded. "Now," she said breathlessly, and broke into a run.

They tore into the underbrush, making a beeline for the boneshaker. As they emerged from the trees, River leapt onto the seat and motioned for Micah to crawl on behind her. She cranked down the pressure lever and took a few seconds to show Micah the frame brackets where he could safely stand without catching his leg in the wheel. By then the pressure was back up. She gunned the engine, and with a roar, they were gone.

Micah held on for dear life as they sped across the frozen plains, swiftly climbing the gentle slopes and then nearly taking flight as they glided down the other side. Every time the weightless feeling came over him, Micah's guts clinched up and he had to fight back the urge to vomit. Any other day, he would have begged River to stop and let him walk. Today, he simply locked his jaw and held on.

A few minutes later, River hit the brakes and spun in a half circle. They came to rest in a cloud of dust along the railroad tracks, facing back towards the river. The dusty road along the tracks led into the forest a mile ahead, and vanished in the shadows. Other than a few birds circling in the sky overhead, they saw no other signs of life.

"What were those things?" River said, still trying to catch her breath.

"They're dead," Micah said in a quaking voice. "Living dead *things*. They walk in those woods."

River set her jaw. "Where is Kale?"

"Back there, in the castle. A few miles up the road-"

"Get off," she said. "Follow the tracks back to the train and explain everything to Socrates."

"No! River, don't go back there!"

"Don't worry about me. Just get the message to Socrates."

"At least take the road," Micah pleaded. "Don't go back into those woods."

She sighed. "All right, I promise. Now go!"

She reached for the throttle, but Micah stopped her with a shout. "Wait!" he called out. "River, wait!"

River pressed her lips together, staring at him. "What is it?"

"They took my drawings. Will you look for my satchel when you get there?"

River rolled her eyes and twisted the throttle. Micah stood staring after her as River kicked up a cloud of dust all the way back to the trees. The sound of the boneshaker echoed in the distance as it disappeared across the old wooden bridge, and then it was gone. Silence fell over the land. Then, as if Micah suddenly realized he was alone and in the open, he turned back down the tracks and began to run, the dull pain of his ankle now barely noticeable and certainly not enough to slow the small man's pace.

Chapter 10

River didn't encounter any more of the undead creatures along the way, but she did find the castle heavily guarded upon her arrival. The portcullis was closed, and River slammed on the brakes as she roared up to the entryway. The boneshaker's rear tire skidded sideways, throwing rocks and dirt into the air, kicking up a cloud of dust that slowly drifted into the forest around her as the boneshaker's steam engine rumbled quietly.

Half a dozen men stood facing her, armed with spears and swords. Twice that number roamed back and forth along the top of the wall. Instead of spears, they carried longbows and crossbows. Two of the guards cautiously approached, eyeing the bone-shaker like some sort of demon. Judging from the looks on their faces, she had frightened them. They didn't know what to think of her, or of her vehicle. That gave River a certain advantage. Even so, she had to be cautious. The last thing she needed was a crossbow bolt through the chest. She pushed the kickstand down and stepped off the boneshaker, watching them closely. As she moved, the two guards tensed up and brandished their spears. River displayed her empty hands.

"Who are you?" one of guards demanded. He was a middle aged man with graying hair and steel blue eyes. His companion was younger and his hair darker, but otherwise shared similar features. River watched them for a moment, sizing them up. They were emaciated, pale of skin and dark around the eyes. Their uniforms were worn, disheveled, and showing patchwork in several places, like clothes that had not only been worn for a lifetime, but had been passed down from one generation to the next. Even their long gray cloaks were weathered and tattered around the edges, and covered with stains and patches. Their weapons were similarly neglected. The shafts of their spears were aged and cracked; the tips sharpened but covered in rust. The same with their swords, and with the weapons of the men on the wall.

"My name is River," she said calmly. "I have come here seeking my companion, a dark-haired warrior named Kale."

"Are you a *Keeper?*" the younger man said.

"A Keeper? What do you mean?"

The guard nodded at the boneshaker. "You journey on the back of a God. You keep his word, do you not?"

River grinned skeptically, not sure if the man was serious. She patted the boneshaker's headlamp. "The boneshaker is not a god, it's a machine. It is powered by steam."

"She's a heretic," his older companion said.

"But her... *machine.*" The younger guard glanced meaningfully at the boneshaker. "This cannot be. It is a test."

"This is a matter for the Keeper," said the second. He looked River up and down. "Come with us."

River frowned. That was a command, not a request. She resisted the urge to reach for her revolver. Obviously, they didn't understand it was a weapon or they probably would have disarmed her already. It was better for now not to attract their attention to it. For the moment, it made sense to go along peacefully, but she bristled at the thought.

"What of my companion?" she said. "Have you seen him or not?" The guards exchanged a glance.

"He is here. You will see him, in time. First you must speak to the Keeper."

"Who is the *Keeper*?"

"Keeper Toolume is the Keeper of the Word, of course."

River started to reply but the older guard silenced her by raising his hand. "You will understand everything in time. Please, follow us."

River nodded her acceptance. The guards signaled for the portcullis to be opened, and they ducked under it as it reached waist-height. River followed them through, and the men on the wall quickly lowered it behind her. On the other side, the guards led River around a protective stone wall that guarded the face of the portcullis from the spears and arrows of invaders. The passageway opened up and River found herself facing the town called Blackstone.

Ancient buildings rose up around her, scattered throughout the area as if they had been cast in their places at random by some archaic god. Narrow alleys and cobbled streets wound between thatch-roofed cottages and two and three story buildings that looked like inns or official government buildings. They were all in similar states of disrepair: the thatched roofs were rotten and collapsing, the paint peeling or altogether gone, and most of the windows were broken or shuttered. The wooden frames on the doors and windows were riddled with termites and crumbling with dry rot.

River saw the keep in the distance, rising over the rooftops. It was a tall stone castle located in the northwestern corner of the town; flanked by two tall towers that commanded views of both the city and the surrounding countryside. She also noticed a set of railroad tracks running along the street in front of the keep and through the town square. They disappeared into an opening in the far section of the wall, which had been crudely boarded up.

The peasants who paused in their work to stare at her as she passed by were gaunt and pale, and even the very young children appeared to be terribly malnourished. Their clothes were in tatters, even worse than the soldiers' uniforms, and many of them had rotten teeth. They seemed to lack even the most basic knowledge of hygiene or nutrition. River gave them pitying looks, which they met with cold hard stares.

The soldiers guided River around the well at the center of town, where she observed a crowd of women and children washing and mending clothes, and collecting water for their homes. She balked at their destitute poverty.

"Everyone here is so thin," she remarked. "Don't you have enough food?"

"We survive," one of the soldiers said.

"But I don't understand. You're surrounded by this forest. You could hunt, farm... your people don't have to live like this."

"The forest belongs to the Ancients," he said impatiently. "Be silent now. No more questions."

His words sounded vaguely like an order and River stiffened ever so slightly. She wasn't accustomed to taking orders from anyone. She cast a glance over her shoulder to see if any of the other guards had followed, and found they had not. For all their show, it was obvious that none of the soldiers truly knew what they were doing. That at least was a small comfort.

She took a deep breath and relaxed, comfortable in the knowledge that the two guards couldn't possibly overwhelm her. If necessary, she'd deal with them and then disappear over the wall before the rest of the guards could even react. That would be an action of last resort, of course. Her first priority was to find Kale and, if at all possible, get him out of there.

At last they reached the keep. The guards led River up the stairs and through the massive wooden doors that stood open at the front of the building. On the way inside, River noticed a wide set of metal rails embedded into the floor, leading into the darkness of the hall. River's eyes still hadn't adjusted to the darkened interior of the keep, and she could only see that they were facing a large room, probably some sort of court.

An elderly man in heavy, light colored robes greeted them. He had a long gray beard and wore his long hood pulled down over his face. He tilted his head sideways, eyeing River up and down, but didn't say a word.

"We've found another intruder," one of the guards said. "Inform the Keeper." The man nodded and then vanished down a long hallway. The guard turned back to his companion. "Remain here until the Keeper is ready, then return to your post."

"Yes, Commander. May the Word protect you."

"And you."

The commander turned and left, leaving River in the company of the young soldier. "Who is the old man?" she asked.

"The Keeper's Thought. He doesn't speak because he's a mute."

"The *Keeper's Thought*? What does he do?"

The guard stared into the distance of the darkened hall. "The Thought is the Keeper's adviser. He is a wise man. He will be an Ancient soon."

"So the Keeper keeps the Word of your god, and the Thought gives the Keeper advice?"

"Is that not as it should be?"

"But you said he's mute. How can he give advice if he can't speak?"

"The Thought sacrificed his tongue for the honor of his position, and for the safety of the Keeper. He does not need to speak for god, does he?"

The soldier's voice had been very monotone at first, as if he'd simply been reciting the same words he'd heard over and over for all of his life. As River questioned him, she noted the pitch of his voice rising, and increasing tension in his posture. The soldier knew what he was supposed to say, as long as nobody asked the wrong questions. The more she tried to fathom the logic of the situation, the more apprehensive he became.

River's shoulders slumped. There was no point trying to make sense out of any of this, she decided. The thing to do was to find Kale, grab him, and run.

She'd kill whoever got in the way. Not that she really wanted to. Looking at these soldiers, it was hard to feel anything but pity. And it wasn't like any of these so-called warriors could really chase her down anyway. They were so starved they'd probably faint before they ran a hundred yards. But Kale's safety was the matter at hand, and if these people presented a threat, she was ready to deal with them.

The "Thought" returned, and made a dismissive gesture to the guard, who saluted, said the words, "May the Word protect you," and then submissively disappeared through the front doors. The old man turned to River, offered a callous smile, and motioned for her to follow him. He proceeded down the hall, and she quickly stepped after him. River was a little surprised that after accompanying her all the way to the keep, the guard seemed to have lost interest in her. If they were willing to leave her alone with the old man, they clearly didn't think of her as much of a threat. River couldn't help feeling slightly insulted, even if their actions would probably make her escape easier.

"Nice place," River said sarcastically, noting the threadbare tapestries hanging on the wall, the rusted sconces, and the worn carpets on the floor. The interior of the castle appeared just as unkempt as the rest of the town. The lack of care and attention were evident in everything she'd seen so far. It was a miracle the town was still standing at all. River couldn't help but wonder how long the townsfolk had been living like this.

The Thought ignored her comment as he led her down the long hall, around a corner, and up a flight of stairs. On the second floor, they entered another long hallway. This time, things appeared more orderly. The black and red rugs that lined the floor showed some wear, but the patterns were bright and the fabric had only a few signs of patchwork. The sconces here were polished brass instead of rusted iron and the paintings and tapestries were, at least, well dusted. Even so, the cool air was heavy with the scent of mildew, and River doubted the rest of the castle would prove any better. They came to a tall wooden door, and the Thought knocked quietly.

"Enter," said a man's voice beyond. The Thought pushed the door open and motioned for River to step inside. She did, and he immediately closed the door behind her.

River found herself in a large, well-appointed room. The tapestries and curtains on the walls here were made of lush fabrics with deep, vibrant colors. Torches burned on the walls and a brass chandelier hung suspended from the ceiling in the middle of the room, casting off the light of dozens of red candles. A polished mahogany desk rested beneath the chandelier, and River noted several inkwells and a stack of yellowing parchment. Two chairs rested before the desk, both matching in quality and design, along with a sofa and several more chairs in the center of the room.

"I would offer you wine, but I'm afraid we had no harvest last year."

River turned to see a figure standing in a nearby doorway. He was a tall, middle-aged man with black hair and beard, and raven-black eyes that sent a chill down her spine. He was dressed in long red and black robes, and moved with an air of authority that demanded respect.

"You're the Keeper?" she said.

"Indeed. I am the Keeper of the Word. That is my title, but my name is Blaise Toolume. Here, you may call me by my name, but in public you must refer to me as *Keeper* or *Keeper Toolume.*"

"My name is River. I've come here for my friend, a warrior who goes by the name of Kale."

"Ah, yes. I know of this man. Most unfortunate. It seems he broke several of our laws, not the least of which was the slaughter of our Ancients. The punishment for this crime is always death."

"Ancients?" said River, her eyes flashing as she remembered what Micah had told her. "You mean the horrible creatures I saw in the forest?"

"You are a stranger here. As such, I will over-look your words, but I urge you to use more caution in the future. Among my people, it is a crime to blaspheme the Ancients."

"Blaspheme? But those creatures... they're dead," River said. "You must see that there's something wrong with those things."

The Keeper set his jaw and fixed her with a dark gaze. "I suggest you heed my warning. You will not get another."

"Fine," River said impatiently. "Then what of my friend? Can I see him now?"

"You may, briefly, but I warn you do not try to free him. His companion escaped this morning. Perhaps you know him? A small man, like a child?"

Silence hung between them, until the Keeper realized River wasn't going to talk. "At any rate," he continued, "Kale must now accept punishment on behalf of his companion as well. Such is the law among my people."

"*Your law?*" River said in an accusing tone.

"God's law, such as it has always been." With that, he snapped his fingers and the door behind them instantly swung open. The Thought stood there, stooped over in the doorway. "Escort our guest to the prison," the Keeper ordered.

The Thought nodded and motioned for River to follow him. She had little choice but to comply.

Chapter 11

River found another guard waiting for her at the front of the keep. He was tall and clean shaven with dark hair, a feature which seemed to be very common in Blackstone. He was in his late thirties and, though his uniform was as tattered as the others' were, it seemed somehow *cleaner,* as if perhaps he took a bit more pride in it than anyone else she had seen. The Thought communicated with the soldier through a series of hand signals, and then disappeared back into the shadows of the building. The guard nodded in her direction.

"My name is Maru Toolume. I am commander of the city watch. I will be your guide while you remain in our town. The Thought has informed me that you wish to visit the prison?"

"Yes," River said. "You said your name is Toolume? Are you the Keeper's son?"

"No, he is my second cousin."

"It's a small town," River mused.

"Indeed. Shall we?"

She scanned the area, wondering just how many people lived there. It couldn't have been more than a thousand. She wondered how long they had all been living like that, closed off to the outside world. It had been decades at least, perhaps even centuries. It occurred to her that malnutrition may not have been the sole cause of the health problems she saw around her. The people of Blackstone may have been breeding in a closed gene pool for too long. Even if they avoided marrying too close, as in the case of cousins, it was still possible for their isolated gene pool to cause certain problems. River had heard of such things before. She sighed as she joined the Commander on the street. They began to walk.

"Tell me about the tracks," she said, nodding toward the rail tracks that ran through the center of town.

"They belong to god. Once, he traveled back and forth on them, surveying the great forest. Now he only rests."

River cocked an eyebrow at that. The first thought that came to mind was that Maru was referring to a locomotive. That didn't make sense, though. No one would mistake a locomotive engine for a god. Would they?

"You've barricaded the walls," she observed. "Is that to keep out the... *the Ancients?*"

"Of course."

"But you worship the Ancients, don't you? Why would you lock them out?"

"The forest belongs to the Ancients. The town is for the living."

"I see. So you fear them?"

Maru fixed his gaze on the street. "It would be blasphemy to say such a thing," he said. "We must protect the Ancients. If we do not, then who will protect us when we join them?"

River froze in her tracks. "Join the Ancients? Are you saying that you will become one of the Ancients?"

"We all must, eventually. Is it not so in your land?"

103

"No," River said absently. "I've never seen... Ancients anywhere else. How does it happen?"

"We die," he said with a shrug. "And then we become Ancients. It is god's will. So says the Keeper, and he should know. He keeps the Word."

"Of course he does," River said absently.

As they resumed their journey, River silently considered Maru's statement. So many things about Blackstone didn't make sense. The entire population was starving, and yet surrounded by a thriving forest, but they refused to hunt or farm the lands around the castle because they belonged to the dead, or as they called them, "Ancients." Stranger still, the people worshipped these undead creatures, and apparently did so at the bidding of some other creature they called "god." A creature that apparently once traveled on the railroad tracks. River couldn't make any sense of it.

Maru took River to one of the northerly towers, which was guarded by two men armed with swords. "Open it," he said as they approached, and one of the guards pulled a key ring from his belt and unlocked the door. They stepped inside and River found herself in a broad, circular room filled with dusty old furniture.

"This way," said Maru. He led River up a flight of circular stairs, past several levels of the tower. Finally, near the top, they entered the prison. The commander pushed the door open and River winced as she stepped inside and noticed the chains and shackles hanging from the walls, and the torture devices scattered throughout the room.

"River!" Kale called out. She glanced across the room and saw the burly warrior in one of the cages near the outside wall. His clothes were rumpled and his hair was a mess, but he seemed no worse for the wear.

"You have five minutes," Maru said. "I will wait here." He closed the door and locked it, standing next to it as River crossed the room. As she did, she took note of everything. Not just the other occupants of the prison, but the layout of the cages and the other pieces of equipment. Anything in the room might prove to be a weapon or tool in the right hands. The trick was to become familiar with everything, and to do it all in a single glance.

"Did Micah find you?" Kale said, latching onto the bars at the front of his cage as she approached him. River nodded ever so slightly, hoping the commander hadn't heard the question. She didn't want to give away any important information.

"Socrates?" Kale said hopefully.

Again, River nodded quietly. Before Kale could ask another incriminating question, she took control of the conversation. "How long have you been in here?"

"Since last night. They arrested us for killing those-"

"Ancients," River interrupted.

"What?"

She quickly explained what she had learned about the Ancients, the Keeper, and their "god." Kale and the others were only partially aware of the city's practices. They knew nothing about the Keeper, the Word, or the Thought until she explained it to them. Or tried, at least. She still hadn't quite grasped the logic that bound their belief system together, and therefore couldn't communicate it very clearly. Then again, the soldier hadn't been able to articulate it very well, either. Perhaps there was a reason for that.

"We have to get out of here," Kale said when she had finished. "These people are insane. They're going to execute us."

"Are you sure?"

"Your friend will have a hearing today," Thane said from the far corner. "Shayla and I have already been sentenced." He stepped out of the corner and River looked him up and down. Thane smiled and offered a hand as he introduced himself.

"I am Thane, bard of Avenston, and the woman over there is my companion, Shayla."

"River Tinkerman," she said, accepting his handshake. River noted that Thane was a tall and vibrantly attractive man, but she found his refinement off-putting. He was good-looking but seemed somehow *delicate*. Such a thing might be said of many of the elfish Tal'mar men, but River had never seen that quality in a human before. It was strange.

"When is the execution planned?" she asked.

"The full moon," said Thane. "It is their tradition. They will light a bonfire in the center of town and burn us as an offering to their clockwork god."

"Clockwork?"

"Aye, the thing is some sort of a machine, but it's like nothing I've ever seen."

That at least, made sense. Perhaps the god truly was a locomotive or an old railcar. "And you say they're going to *burn you?*"

Thane nodded grimly. "Aye, so their god commanded."

River closed her eyes and took a deep breath. She felt the weight of her revolver on her hip and sensed the watch commander's presence at the far end of the room. She didn't necessarily have to kill him, just one shot to the leg or shoulder would be enough. He'd give up the keys without a fight. Then she could open the cages, and they could climb out the window. Devils, they could even walk out the front gate if they really wanted to. There wasn't a true warrior in the entire town. They were all haggard, untried peasants. River doubted any one of them would stand up to Kale with his swords, and certainly not against River's revolver.

But something held her back. Perhaps it was her reluctance to draw innocent blood. After all, the guardsmen may have been coconspirators, but the truth was that they were just ignorant fools. Ignorant and superstitious. How else could she explain their worship of the undead creatures they called Ancients? And what about this *god,* this clockwork machine that Thane had referred to? River knew she could get Kale out of town and never look back, but she *had to know* the answers to the questions plaguing her.

No, she wasn't ready to leave just yet. Besides, she wasn't about to abandon the boneshaker that she had spent so many weeks painstakingly recreating. She'd wait a while. Then, only if it was absolutely necessary, she would help Kale and the others escape. Hopefully, Socrates would find them before then. After all, Micah must have returned by now. All Socrates had to do was guide the *Horse* down the tracks and right into town.

Chapter 12

It was early evening when Maru returned to the tower. He was flanked by two guards wearing swords and helmets, and he carried a key ring in his right hand.

"It is time," was all he said, and that was all he needed to say. Kale had been waiting for this moment ever since River left. He'd begged her then to help him escape, but she wouldn't hear of it. For some reason, River told him to be patient. That was ridiculous, of course. Patience was for card games, not for life and death situations. Unfortunately, River was the one on the outside, and therefore she was the one making the decisions. Kale had no choice but to go along with her plans, however ridiculous they might be.

Kale glanced at Thane as the guards checked his shackles. The bard's face was unreadable. When the guards were satisfied, they pushed Kale out of the cage and guided him towards the door.

"May your ancestors watch over you," Thane called out behind him.

Kale glanced at Shayla as he passed her cell, and got his first glimpse of the woman up close. She was quite attractive, with olive skin and mysterious hazel eyes, and auburn hair that perfectly framed her face. Her lips were full, pouty, and surprisingly red, considering she hadn't had access to face paints in at least a week. Her long, lightly curled hair swooped gently down over her shoulders to fall across ample breasts, and her tight leather bodice drew his eyes involuntarily to her thin figure.

With some effort, Kale drew his gaze up to meet Shayla's, and he saw a wicked smile curling up the corners of her lips. Somehow, Kale instinctively knew Shayla was trouble. Perhaps more trouble than everything else combined. Naturally, that only made her that much more intriguing. Kale immediately decided that not only was he *not* going to be executed, but he was also going to rescue her, and in doing so, earn her eternal gratitude.

One of the guards ended these thoughts by rapping Kale on the back of the head with a sword pommel. Kale moaned and rubbed his head, and Shayla's voice rang out in laughter. As the guard pushed him into the stairwell, Kale risked another thumping. He paused to look directly at her and in a low, devilish voice said, "I'll be back, gorgeous."

"I'll be waiting, hero," Shayla said in a tantalizing voice.

Kale disappeared into the hall and the guards slammed the door behind him. Kale and the guards disappeared down the stairwell, and the prison chamber went silent

"I think that one likes you," Thane said, grinning, staring at Shayla.

"That's what I get paid for," she said. "To make 'em like me. Though I must admit, I might let that one *like me* for free. The first time, at least."

Thane laughed aloud as Shayla smiled thoughtfully.

Maru led Kale out of the tower and through the front entrance of the keep, where they found River waiting. She joined them as they passed through the set of tall wooden doors into the long, dimly lit courtroom. The grand hall was empty now, save for the row of unlit urns lined up near the end of the room, and the red velvet curtains that hung at the far wall. A few torches burned along the outside walls, making shadows leap and dance across the stone floor. A small crowd of gawkers followed after them, and fanned out across the back of the hall.

"Your hearing is to be public," River whispered, glancing over her shoulder at the onlookers.

Kale gazed into her face. "Is that good?"

"I don't think they'll be any help."

Maru turned to face Kale, his countenance little more than a silhouette in the darkened chamber. "I have warned your friend River, and I will warn you likewise: do not speak until god asks it of you. Do not argue or attempt to defend yourself. Wait until you are questioned. Speak honestly, for if you do not, god will know."

Kale glanced at River and found her distracted. She was staring at the curtains at the end of the room. The guards slammed the doors shut behind them and simultaneously doused the torches. The room became pitch black. The old man called *the Thought* appeared before them waving an incense burner that gave off a faint red glow. Smoke rolled out of the burner like a fog as he passed before the crowd and circled the room, stopping at last to set the burner before the urns. He then disappeared into the shadows.

"Follow me," Maru commanded, striding forward. He led Kale and River through the smoke, which gave off a sickly-sweet odor like that of an overripe fruit. They blinked their watering eyes as they approached the unlit urns and stopped a few feet before them. The shadows beyond seemed to part, and the Keeper came walking towards them from the corner of the room. He raised his right hand and a torch flared to life.

"From the dawn of days to the breaking of the world, the sacred Keepers have maintained the torch of god. Now in these darkest of days, I -the sacred Keeper of the Word- bring forth the light!"

He touched the torch to the first burner and it instantly burst into flames. The fire leapt from one to the next, until they were all alight. The Thought appeared at his side and accepted the torch from the Keeper. He raised it high into the air, and in response, the curtains at the end of the room parted. At last, the flickering, dancing firelight fell across the clockwork god.

It was a machine of steel and brass and copper that to River strangely resembled the visage of a human face. Pipes and steel beams formed the shapes of eyes and a mouth, as well as two arm-like appendages that sprouted out from each side. Through the gleaming metal, River and Kale glimpsed many gears, cogs, and springs. Rising out of the machine's head was a tall bronze smokestack. To her surprise, River saw something at the center of it all that resembled a large gyroscope, but in the dim light she couldn't be certain.

"And now," the Keeper announced in a loud voice, "God will awaken."

He stepped around the flaming urns and walked up to the machine, pausing to bow reverently before it. Then he stepped around the side and disappeared behind the curtains. They heard the telltale creak of a door opening, and Kale and River exchanged a glance.

"Did he just crawl inside?" Kale said in a whisper.

River nodded, half-grinning with disbelief. In the distance, they heard the sound of the Keeper closing and latching the door, and then getting himself settled inside. Then, with the flick of a switch, the clockwork god came to life. Two crude electric lights came on in the openings that resembled eyes. There was a hiss, followed by a vapor of steam that washed out into the room like a fog. The arms rose and fell twice, and then the mouth began to move.

"Great warrior from distant lands," a voice said, it sounded very much like the Keeper speaking through a long section of pipe: "You stand accused of breaking our sacred laws and slaughtering the Ancients. What say you?"

"You've got to be kidding," Kale said, shaking his head. "Keeper, what are you doing?"

"BLASPHEMER!" the voice shouted. "I AM NOT THE KEEPER, I AM THE WORD!"

"But we saw you get in-" Kale started, but River elbowed him in the ribs.

"Just play along," she whispered. Kale rolled his eyes.

"All right, all right," he said in an irritated tone. "You are the *Word*. I plead *not guilty*."

"You may plead for your life, or nothing!" shouted the machine.

Kale shook his head and looked at River. He was clearly running out of patience with the charade. The look on his face said *Can't we just kill him now?*

River mouthed the word "No," and shook her head. Kale clenched his jaw but said no more.

"In one day, at the lighting of the bonfire, you shall be my sacrifice," said the machine. "Meanwhile, in recompense for your escaped companion, you will suffer thirty lashes in the public square. The sentence is to be carried out immediately."

"That's not fair!" Kale shouted. "I can't control someone else's actions."

"No, but you can prevent them," said the machine. Then, with a clunking sound, the mouth closed, the arms went back into place, and the lights went dim. The clockwork "god" had once again returned to sleep. After a moment of scuffling, the Keeper reappeared from behind the curtains.

"God has spoken!" he said loudly, so that the witnesses at the back of the room could hear. "Let the sentence be carried out!"

Two guards stepped forward and caught Kale by the arms. He began to struggle, so they pulled him off balance and dragged him backwards from the room. The rest of the crowd closed in around them as they exited the building and headed for the town square. River trailed along behind, fingering the handle of her revolver.

Kale fought the guards as they dragged him down the street, and for a moment, River almost thought he might escape. As he regained his footing,

Kale twisted around, yanking back on his chains. One of the guards stumbled forward and Kale slammed his fist into the guard's face. The man dropped like a rock.

The second guard released his grip on the chains and went for his sword. Kale was faster. He leapt on the guard, forcing him backwards, and the man stumbled to the ground. Kale reached for the handle of the sword, still locked in its scabbard, just as someone booted him in the face. Kale rolled aside, dazed as the crowd closed in.

The next few seconds were a flurry. River saw the townsfolk leap to the defense of the guards. They lifted Kale up into the air and carried him the rest of the way to the square. There, just a few yards from the well, they separated. Four watchmen took hold of his chains and spread out, holding Kale's arms out to the sides. He was utterly defenseless. The guard Kale had punched reappeared, now brandishing a long bullwhip. The crowd pulled back, giving him room to carry out the sentence. Kale struggled against his bonds in futility. As weak as the soldiers were, he was no match against four of them, much less the entire town.

"Think you're clever, eh?" the guard said, raising the whip handle into the air. "I'm going to teach you a lesson."

He hauled back to swing. At the same instant, River's hand flashed to the handle of her revolver. In a fraction of a second, she drew the weapon and fired. Her instinctive aim was deadly accurate. The bullet struck the guard in the hand. He let out a painful yelp and dropped the whip. Terrified voices rose in a clamor around him as the guard clutched at his bleeding appendage. He turned, confused, trying to ascertain what exactly had just happened. His eyes widened as he gaze settled on River, and he saw the weapon in her hand.

"I told you she was a god!" someone shouted. Another soldier stepped forward, and River recognized him as the young guard she had encountered at the city gate.

"I'm not a god," she said tersely. "But I'm a damn fine shot. The next person who touches that whip is gonna get a bullet in the chest, instead of the hand."

Off to the side, another guard let out a cry as he drew his sword and rushed her. River leveled the revolver and fired. The man screamed as he fell to the ground, clutching a wound bleeding in his shoulder. His sword clattered harmlessly across the stones. River turned slowly, training her weapon on various people in the crowd.

"Don't make me kill you," she said. "I will if I have to." She turned her attention to the men holding Kale's chains.

"Release him," she ordered.

There was a scuffling as one of the guards brought forth the keys and removed Kale's shackles. Kale hurried to her side, massaging his wrists.

"I knew you wouldn't let them do it," he said, grinning.

"I shouldn't have done that. Socrates won't be happy. You remember what he said about respecting other cultures."

"He's not the one they were going to sacrifice." Kale turned slowly as the crowd closed in around them. "What are we gonna do now?" he said.

"We're going to leave."

River grabbed Kale's arm and began walking down the street, into the crowd. She held the revolver high with her finger on the trigger, but no one moved to make way for them. Out of nowhere, the Keeper appeared. Apparently, he had been watching from the crowd.

"She has a powerful weapon," he shouted, "but she is only one. We are many! She can't kill us all."

"You're right about that," River said, training her sights on him. "But I can make sure you're first."

The Keeper stood frozen in front of her. River could see him calculating his next move. He couldn't back down, not now. He was the Keeper of the Word. He was the mysterious voice of god from the clockwork machine. The Keeper had gambled everything by stepping forward. If he relented now, the townsfolk would think him weak.

River saw his gaze flash to her revolver and she smiled grimly.

"Don't even think it," she said. "You're not that fast."

They stood there for a few seconds in a tense standoff, frustration oozing from the crowd around them. River had the uneasy feeling that events had just spiraled out of her control. Suddenly, there was no scenario in which everything could come out all right. The Keeper couldn't back down -not without losing the respect of his followers- but neither could River.

"This wasn't how things were supposed to go," she muttered.

"You did the right thing," Kale said. "They were going to kill me."

"No, they were going to *whip you*. Now they want to kill us both, and it's my fault. Look at them. They don't even understand."

"I don't care... better them than us."

River's guts twisted up as she thought of the innocent, ignorant townsfolk around her. The last thing she wanted to do was kill them. It wasn't their fault that they believed the Keeper's lies. If only they knew... if only there were some way to show them the truth about their Keeper and his phony god. But how?

A deep mournful howl rang out, and River's heart leapt at the distant sound of the *Iron Horse's* steam whistle. Around her, the crowd shuffled nervously. They stared at the treetops over the castle walls, searching for the source of that unearthly noise. Kale clapped his hand on her shoulder and began to laugh.

The moment of distraction was all that the Keeper needed. He made a subtle gesture, and two guards leapt out of the crowd. They tackled the couple from behind, driving them both to the ground in an instant. River tried to roll over to defend herself, but the crowd closed in around her, and she felt a boot press down on her back. Another attacker stepped on her hand, crushing it around the grip of her revolver. At the same time, someone put a sharpened blade to her throat.

"All right!," River grunted under the crushing weight of her attackers. "I give up!"

She released her grip on the revolver and it vanished from sight. Her attackers hoisted her up and quickly shackled her arms behind her back. All the while, that cold sharp blade rested against her throat, ready to slice her open at the first sign of resistance. Out of the corner of her eye, she saw Kale. He was in very much the same predicament.

Within minutes, the couple found themselves back in the tower, locked in separate cells. River was in the cell Micah had occupied, and Kale was back in with Thane.

"The god's luck," Thane said. "Shayla and I had hoped at least you had found freedom. Now no one will live to sing our ballads."

"It was my fault," River said. "I shouldn't have let my guard down. Not even for a second."

"Alas fair maid, at least I will die easier having looked upon your beauty." River blushed at Thane's compliment.

"Pay no attention to him," Shayla said. "He's got a silver tongue but a heart of cheap brass. Once he beds you, he'll be off on his next adventure without so much as a *Thank You.*"

"Lies!" Thane protested. "I assure you, my intentions are nothing but honorable. Though, I'll admit I cursed Kale once or twice for leaving us here to rot, but I was certain he had at least made an escape. Shayla saw that much through the window."

"Coming back here wasn't my idea," Kale said, making a sour face. Then he hastily added, "I would have come back to rescue you later, of course."

"Of course," Thane said dryly.

"Well he did promise as much," Shayla said, grinning. "Didn't you, my hero?"

Kale reddened slightly and River arched an eyebrow as she saw the look that passed between the two of them.

"No matter," Thane said, changing the subject. "We're all in the same kettle now. By this time tomorrow, they'll be prepping the bonfire to cook us."

The *Iron Horse's* whistle sounded again in the distance, and a smile came to River's lips.

"I'm not so sure about that," she said. "I think things are about to get a lot more complicated for the Keeper."

The whistle blew several more times over the next half hour. Soon, it was accompanied by the deep, drumming sound of the massive locomotive engine. The noise built up to a roar, and the whistle howled as the *Iron Horse* bore down on the castle. As it grew nearer, the tracks in the street began to vibrate. The townsfolk gathered in the square, murmuring fearfully as they touched the tracks and felt the *Horse's* ominous approach.

Shayla, who was located next to the window overlooking the street, described the entire scene. The Keeper sent guards to calm the townsfolk, but even the guards lost all sense of composure as the noise built up to a wild crescendo. The peasants began running back and forth, wailing and moaning about the fury of their god, some even calling on the Keeper to defend them from his wrath.

Then at last, the *Horse* plowed through the castle wall in a fury of splintered wood and shattered stone, and the crowd scattered to the winds. Only the Keeper remained, watching with dark, calculate-ing eyes as the locomotive roared into the town square. Immediately, the brakes locked up. The shrieking sound rattled the streets and rooftops, and sparks rained down on the square. Finally, the *Iron Horse* came to a stop. There was a loud hiss as the engineer released the built up steam pressure and the brakes locked into place. The scene became eerily quiet.

"Someone's coming out now," Shayla said, describing the scene to the others from her vantage near the window. "He's strange looking, like a man but covered in fur."

"That would be Socrates," Kale said, grinning.

"He's walking to the front of the locomotive. A crowd is gathering, but he's just standing there, looking down at them. Oh, my-"

"What is it?" Thane demanded. "What's going on?"

Shayla drew her gaze away from the window and turned to face her companions. "The towns-folk... they're worshipping Socrates."

Chapter 13

Keeper Toolume stepped bravely out in front of the crowd.

"Greetings, honored one! I am Blaise Toolume, Keeper of the Word."

Socrates eyed the man up and down and then drew his gaze along the street. He noted the impoverished peasants bowing down to him like a god, and the watchmen scattered throughout the crowd, hands uneasily resting on their weapons. Socrates fixed his gaze on the well for a moment, studying it curiously, and then turned his attention back to the Keeper.

"I am Socrates, engineer and commander of the *Iron Horse*. I understand you are holding one of my crewmen in your stockade?"

"Most regrettably, this is true. You may meet with him at your convenience, of course. In the meanwhile, we will begin preparations for a great feast in your honor."

The Keeper raised his voice at this last part, as if to make sure everyone in town could hear. Instantly, the street became a flurry of activity. The ignorant worshippers abandoned their prostrations and hurried off to perform their duties. Socrates leapt off the front of the *Horse* and thumped heavily to the ancient cobblestones. He raised himself upright, stretching his shirt and vest across his massive simian chest, and a slight whirring sound emanated from his body. With obvious trepidation, the Keeper approached him.

"My crewman?" Socrates said, immediately dispensing with any notion of small talk.

"Of course, this way if you please."

*

Shayla described the scene to her companions and then fell silent as Socrates followed the Keeper into the tower. A minute later, Socrates entered the jail alone. He took a moment to size up the situation, and then fixed his gaze on River.

"I should have known I would find you here, too," he said.

"Sorry, Socrates. I was just trying to help Kale."

"Despite having the best of intentions, you've managed to do exactly the opposite. The two of you," he glanced back and forth between them, "have made a mess of things. Are you unharmed?"

"Just a few bruises," Kale said. "Although the Keeper is planning to execute us tomorrow."

"What were you thinking?" Socrates said angrily as he began pacing between their cages. "What was the first thing I told you, on the day we left Sanctuary?"

"To follow orders and respect others," River said quietly.

"Exactly! I warned you that not only would crew members have different beliefs, but that we might encounter cultures that seemed strange or even repulsive."

"But you don't understand," Kale argued.
"These people worship the dead."

"And a false god," River added. "It's a machine controlled by the Keeper. The whole thing is a sham. And these peasants are too ignorant and frightened to see through it. We had to do something."

"I have heard Micah's stories of the dead," Socrates said. "We will discuss this later. Tell me now about this *god*."

River and Kale began talking at once, tripping over each other to get the story out. By the time they finished fleshing out the details, Socrates had stopped pacing to stare distantly out the window, stroking his chin. River almost thought she heard the mechanicals inside his skull speed up as he focused his thoughts.

"I'm not sure where it came from, but I do know that it's a machine," River said. "What we need to do is destroy the thing, so the whole town can see what their god really is."

"And what do you suppose that will accomplish?" said Socrates. "What do you think it would do to these people, who have spent their entire lives worshipping that piece of machinery?"

River glanced at Kale. "At least they would know," she said. "They have a right to know."

"So they do, but is it our place to do this? There's no telling what these people might do when their leader is exposed. They might turn away from their beliefs, or instead they might turn on us. Our entire crew might be in danger. Unfortunately, it seems we have little choice at this point. Give me some time to work out a plan."

"Don't take too much time," Kale said. "I'd rather not become a pot roast."

"My advice would be to think before you jump into the kettle next time." Socrates turned away from them and headed for the door.

"You're not going to get us out of here?" River said. "Socrates!"

He paused in front of the door. "No, River. I am not." The guard opened the door and Socrates entered the stairwell with the sound of River's curses echoing in his ears. Kale settled down in his cell and shot her a vicious grin.

"Now you know how it feels," he said sarcastically. River fixed him with a menacing glare and Kale's grin vanished.

Chapter 14

Socrates left the tower, ambling past the well on his way back to the *Horse*. With the excitement past, the women of the town had assembled around the square to finish their laundry and other chores. Socrates was among them before they even realized it, and suddenly they began to cry out and fall to their knees.

"Stop!" he called out. "Do not subjugate yourselves to me. I am not a god."

"But lord," one woman said cautiously, still bowing down low. "You are like our god, and you ride the rails, just as he once did."

"And your steed!" cried out another. "You ride a great powerful beast that breathes smoke and fire."

"My steed, as you call it, is a machine," said Socrates. "It is a collection of moving parts, built by human hands, much like this well." To demonstrate, he cranked the handle, lowering the bucket into the well. After it filled, he brought it back up and helped himself to a long drink.

"You drink our water?" the first woman said. Slowly and uncertainly, she rose to her feet. "Then you are truly not a god?"

"I am not."

"But your steed... your *machine*. Is it not like you?"

Socrates scratched his head, considering how to best answer. It was impossible to deny, considering the machinery under his skin was clearly visible. Yet, how could he make the ignorant creature understand?

"Yes, I am a machine, but I have consciousness, whereas most machines do not."

"Consciousness?"

Socrates sighed. "I think. I reason and feel. A machine cannot do these things."

"But you are a machine."

"We are all machines, of a sort," Socrates said impatiently. "We are made of moving parts. But if we have consciousness, then we are more than the sum of our parts."

"Then we are gods?"

Socrates grimaced, wondering if it was better to let her believe that or not. Unfortunately, there was no easy way to communicate these abstract concepts to uneducated peasants. He might as well have been describing steam engines or static electricity. Apparently, they already believed these things were magical anyway.

"It is not for me to tell you who or what god is," he said at last. "These things you must decide for yourself. I for one, will not worship a creature made by human hands."

He left, before she could ask another question and send the conversation spinning even deeper into uncontrollable territory. Socrates climbed back a-board the *Iron Horse* and went to his laboratory, located in the upper half of a large two-story car about a quarter mile back. Along the way, he en-countered numerous crewmembers. They all had questions, but he waved them off with the promise of an announcement to come shortly. His last order just before leaving the train had been for the entire crew to remain aboard. For now, he was satisfied to keep that order in place. Until he knew more about Blackstone, its people and its culture, it would be best to limit interactions.

It was also best, he thought grimly, that the Keeper didn't know just how small his crew actually was. The situation as it stood was more like a game of pawns than anything else. Socrates needed to understand the Keeper and his subjects in order to anticipate their next movements. If he succeeded at that, then he'd be able to think several steps ahead. The fact that the *Iron Horse* and her crew were a mystery gave him the upper hand. Better to keep it that way until the matter was settled. But first, he had a different mystery to solve.

Socrates didn't have the capacity to burn calories or store energy, but his maker had designed the simian automaton with the abilities to eat and drink superficially like a human. After securing the door in the lab, he removed the unprocessed well water from the copper storage vessel in his belly by urinating into a glass. Once that was done, Socrates fired up a burner and prepared several vials for testing.

As the burner warmed, Socrates placed a long coil of copper tubing on the table and attached it to several brass fittings and glass containers, creating primitive distillation and osmosis chambers. The entire process, if it worked, was intended to remove the impurities from the well water so he could analyze them. It was admittedly a shot in the dark, but not entirely uneducated. For the moment, Socrates simply wanted to prove a theory.

A short while later, the steam-powered engineer gathered five crewmembers to join him for the feast. They were unarmed, which Socrates intended to be a show of confidence. The Keeper had already seen River's boneshaker, as well as her revolver (which apparently he had in his possession, somewhere) and had also seen the *Iron Horse* in all her majestic glory. This left little room for doubt that Socrates and his crew were in possession of superior fire-power and technology. Showing up to the feast completely unarmed would demonstrate to the Keeper as well as his subjects that Socrates and his crew had nothing to fear. Conversely, it would fuel speculation among the townsfolk that perhaps the Keeper wasn't very powerful at all. If the Keeper of their god's Word couldn't strike fear into the heart of these strangers, then was he worthy of fear at all?

Socrates saw these thoughts fleeting across the faces of the townsfolk as he walked past them and climbed the stairs into the keep that evening. He grinned inwardly and thought, *The first seeds of doubt have been sown. Now to watch them grow...*

Socrates noted the strange rails on the floor as he entered the main hall, but said nothing as the Keeper hurried to welcome him. The rest of the room was brightly lit by dozens of candles and torches that illuminated a long heavily laden table in the center of the room. At the end of the room, Socrates saw the two curtains that hung down over the face of his host's god.

"My esteemed guests!" the Keeper said, welcoming Socrates and his companions. "I am so pleased that you have joined us. Socrates, as my guest of honor, I insist that you take the seat at the head of table. Your men may sit alongside you, as you wish."

"You are most considerate," Socrates replied. "But it would only be fitting for you, my kind host, to sit at my right hand."

"As you wish."

Socrates couldn't help but note that the Keeper was going out of his way to show no fear of the ape and his men. He took a long look around the room as he settled into the chair facing the curtains. Socrates felt an overwhelming curiosity about the clockwork god hidden behind them, but couldn't act on it for the moment. His attention fell to the ancient, handcrafted table and chairs. Socrates knew from the wear on their finish that all of the furnishings were older than anyone in the room, save perhaps for himself. It was equally probable that the art of building such fine furniture had been completely lost to previous generations.

The table and chairs were ancient, but aging poorly. They hadn't been properly maintained. The wood should have been cleaned, oiled, and polished regularly. The lack of proper maintenance was evident in the dry, crackled finish and the rather large cracks in the tabletop that the servants had attempted to conceal with tablecloths.

He studied the shabbily dressed servants who brought food to the table, and even studied the food itself, a banquet of roast pheasant, freshly baked bread, and vegetables. Socrates learned something from every detail. Even from halfway across the table Socrates could see the vegetables were stunted and the pheasants were small and lacking in fat;

most likely wild birds from the forest captured as they landed inside the city walls. This, sadly, was probably a better meal than most of the peasants ever had.

The bread loaves were small and likely full of seeds and stones. Amateur cook that he was, this was a particular affront to the gorilla. The stunted growth of the pheasants and vegetables perhaps couldn't be helped, but there was never any excuse for poorly made bread. If he accomplished nothing else during his stay, Socrates intended to educate the peasants on this matter.

"Wine?" the Keeper said, displaying a bottle with a flourish. "I'm afraid the bad weather has depleted our supply, but I always keep a few bottles in reserve."

"Thank you," said Socrates, holding up his glass.

"I hope you find the food satisfactory. This was once a lush farmland, but for many generations we have suffered with too few crops and too many hungry bellies."

"The forest outside your wall seems fertile," Socrates said.

"Ah, perhaps, but it does not belong to us."

"So I have heard."

The Keeper leaned closer and lowered his voice.

"Do not think less of us because we are ignorant. My people are simple, but I guide them gently, like a shepherd."

"No doubt you do. However, it has been my experience that the ignorant always hunger for knowledge, just as your people's bellies hunger for food."

"Ah, but is that not the way of things?" The Keeper took a sip of his wine and smiled. "Alas, we have no control over the world, or we would solve all of these problems with a snap of our fingers."

"Would you?" Socrates said.

"Of course! What sort of man would let his people starve unnecessarily?"

"Indeed. In that case, it may interest you to know that I have analyzed the water in your city's well and found it tainted."

The Keeper blinked. His mask of congeniality vanished for a moment and Socrates was sure the man was genuinely surprised.

"My people have been drinking from that well for generations," he said uncomfortably. "For a thousand years or more..."

"The contamination is mild," Socrates said. "It is not the sort of thing one would notice. However, the effect is cumulative."

"I see... I'm afraid you'll have to explain this to me in greater detail. You have an understanding of things that, unfortunately, are beyond me."

Socrates glanced at his companions and found the other men greedily eating the portions on their plates. Several had finished their wine, and a servant began refilling their glasses.

"The contamination is a rare element known in my country as *Starfall*. The source of it appears to have been extraterrestrial... a meteor that struck our planet a thousand years ago, and in the process scattered this toxic element far and wide."

The Keeper laughed loudly. "A poison that fell from the sky? Is that what you'd have us believe?"

"I didn't say it was a poison, though I assure you it can kill. It can also have other *unfortunate* side-effects."

"Aha! So you say our well is contaminated with some *thing* that fell from the heavens and now does what? Makes us grow old, perhaps?" The Keeper laughed at his own cleverness, deliberately mocking Socrates. The ape, being far too intelligent to be insulted, simply stared at him.

"Starfall is an energizing agent of some sort," he explained patiently. "It can burn like coal for months, or even years. It can alter the structural behavior of iron and copper. It can even alter living things."

"Now that is quite a fairy tale," the Keeper said, raising his glass. "A toast to our guest, the esteemed traveler and storyteller."

The rest of the guests raised their glasses, shouting, "Hear, hear!"

Once the room had quieted, Socrates fixed the Keeper with a serious gaze.

"How long have you known?"

"Whatever do you mean?"

"This is not the time for flowery speech, Keeper. I know what you have behind the curtains. I also know what causes your dead to walk. You know these things as well, do you not?"

The Keeper's smiled faded and his eyes grew dark.

"Believe me when I tell you *machine,* that your only option is to get back on that 'Iron Horse' of yours and leave my town."

"I won't be the last," Socrates said. "We are the first of many who will come. If you drive us away, you might protect your city for another year, possibly even five, but eventually they will come, and they will overwhelm you. They will seek Starfall at first, as I do, but others will come seeking wealth and glory. They will come to discover and document, and to conquer. They will marry your daughters and entice your sons away, and if you are not prepared, your city will fade into obscurity."

"I think not!" the Keeper shouted. He lifted the dagger next to his plate and stabbed it into the table menacingly. The room around them went silent.

"I see an entirely different future," he snarled. "I'll arrest you and your crew, and I'll put you to work serving my kinsmen. Then I'll bury your vehicle and dismantle those tracks. You will disappear and no one will ever know what became of you. The Ancients will protect us, and stories of them will spread to kingdoms far and wide. Fear and respect will keep trespassers out of my forest for another thousand years!"

He was shouting by the time he finished, and several guards had approached the table with their swords drawn. Socrates glanced at his companions just in time to see one of them drop forward onto his plate, unconsciousness.

"Move, you fools!" he shouted, leaping from his chair. "You've been drugged!"

One of the other crewmen tried to rise, but instead knocked over his glass and fell out of his chair. The others seemed to have fallen asleep. The guards rushed at Socrates but he spun, twisting away from a drawn sword, and closed his grip around the guard's hand. He squeezed, and the guard screamed as the bones in his hand snapped like twigs. The guard fell to his knees.

Socrates was on his feet. He caught the edge of the table and used it to balance his weight as he threw his legs in the air, kicking at his next attacker. His feet hammered the guard's chest and threw him backwards across the room. Another soldier closed in brandishing a rusted old rapier. Socrates lifted the disabled attacker from the floor and used his opponent's body as a shield. In his haste, the soldier thrust his sword right through the poor man's chest.

After that, they closed in around him. Socrates lost count as he spun around, kicking and punching with his long simian limbs. He was a machine, a tireless fighter, but the numbers of his enemy were simply overwhelming. It was only a matter of time.

Eventually, they managed to tackle him from behind and drive him to the ground. After that, Socrates had no leverage to continue the fight. The guards shackled him, and for good measure, locked a collar around his throat. Then, when they were satisfied that he couldn't escape, the Keeper ordered Socrates locked in the tower with his companions.

As the guards dragged Socrates from the room, he heard the Keeper's voice shouting "To the train!"

Chapter 15

The guards took Socrates and his companions to the tower and locked them up with the others. They placed the unconscious crewmen in a single cell, and left them to sleep off their stupor. Socrates they caged alone, with his wrists shackled behind his back and his ankles chained to the floor. One of the men touched the patch of bare metal and gears on Socrates' head curiously, and Socrates roared and lunged against the chains. The man fell over backwards in his scramble to get away. After that, the guards hurriedly locked the cages and left the room.

"You should have known better than to trust the Keeper," River said, watching Socrates test his bonds.

"I did what I must," Socrates replied. "I was morally obligated to give the Keeper every opportunity to do the right thing. Now that I have told him the truth and seen his response, I no longer owe him anything."

"That sense of honor won't save you from the pyre, strange one," Thane said. "The Keeper and his ancestors have held this village trapped in superstitious fear for centuries. That is power he won't give up easily."

Socrates moved slowly, pulling at his chains, testing their strength.

"Can you break free?" River said. Instead of answering, Socrates braced his legs apart as far as the chains would allow. Then he roared and threw his arms out to his sides, giving a massive heave against the chains. As the chain that bound his wrists went taught, the shackles on his wrists burst open and fell to the floor. Shayla gasped, and Thane stepped forward, eyes wide.

"I think the Keeper may have underestimated your companion," Thane whispered to Kale in a low voice.

Socrates rolled his shoulders, testing the movement of his limbs. Nothing appeared damaged. River pressed her face to the bars in her cage. "Socrates, are you going to break us out of here?"

"One thing at a time," he said. "The chains on my legs are much heavier, and the bars on this cage..." He stepped forward to examine them. "I believe escape is possible, given enough time."

"All that massive strength," Shayla observed thoughtfully. "You allowed them to capture you, didn't you? Why?"

"I already explained why," Socrates muttered. "I went to the Keeper in trust, and he betrayed me. Everyone in this town saw that."

"Ah, and so now they will question their leader's honesty, is that it?" said Thane.

"I'm sure they already had," said Socrates. "I have simply provided evidence to the fact."

"Subversive," Thane said in a tone of admiration. "You are a dangerous political opponent."

Socrates thumped down on the floor next to his leg chains and gave them a tug, testing their strength. They were considerably heavier and stronger

136

than the ones on his wrist had been. The weak spot remained the same in both cases: the shackles. He fumbled around his rib cage for a moment, locating a hidden switch, and pressed it. The side of his rib cage swung open, revealing a section of ribs made from iron or some other blackish metal, and just beneath, a small chamber filled with tools. Socrates reached into his torso and withdrew a small tool with multiple screwdriver-like attachments. He began fumbling with the locks on his ankles, and Kale let out a cheer.

"I should've known you'd have a backup plan," he said.

"Being prepared is not the same as having a plan," Socrates said wisely. "I had no way of knowing the Keeper wasn't an honorable man, nor could I possibly have known he'd lock me in this tower with the rest of you. It was simply a matter of probabilities... and the fact that I already keep these tools with me for maintenance purposes. I am a machine, you realize."

"So you are," Thane said. "And yet unlike any other I've ever seen. Who created you?"

"I'm afraid that is a story for another time," Socrates said as the shackle on his right leg opened. He tossed it aside and quickly began working on the second. They heard shouting outside the window and River turned her attention to Shayla.

"What's going on out there?"

Shayla pressed herself up to the bars, straining for a clear view of the street below. "The Keeper's guards are clearing your train. It looks like he means to arrest your entire crew."

"That is acceptable," said Socrates. "I suspected he would either arrest them, or send them off. His choices in the matter were somewhat limited."

"Acceptable?" River said loudly. "Socrates, you can't let the Keeper do this!"

"And how would you stop him?"

"Open this cage and I'll show you!"

Socrates shook his head. "No. I will not open your cage. Not yet." He shook his chains free and stepped to the back of his cell. He complacently settled down on the straw and reclined, resting his head on one arm. "The Keeper is following the path of least resistance. By arresting our crew, he can make sure no one knows what became of us. At the same time, he can breathe new life into the town's gene pool. From what I have seen, they need it."

"Devils!" Kale cursed, slamming his arm into the cage. "Have you gone mad? Do something!"

"I will not. Nor will you. Rest assured, I will not let the Keeper execute you... any of you. But for now, we must let certain actions take their natural course. I suggest you all get some rest. Tomorrow will be a busy day."

Socrates leaned his head back and closed his eyes. Thane stared at the ape in disbelief, and then turned to Kale. "Your friend could rescue us, but instead he naps? I'm afraid I don't understand."

"Neither do I," Kale said bitterly. "Socrates, get up! Get us out of here!"

In the shadowy corner of his cell, Socrates remained still, and for all appearances, seemed to doze off. Halfway across the room, River frowned and wondered if a machine could sleep. It was but one more uncertainty to add to those she'd been harboring about Socrates.

They continued shouting and taunting the gorilla until their voices went hoarse. By then it was late, and one by one, they settled down on the straw-covered stones to fall into a fitful, uncomfortable sleep.

Chapter 16

Rose-colored sunlight slanted through the window and into River's cell as her eyes fluttered open. The chill of dawn was in the air, and a silence lay upon the town. She crawled to her feet, stretching out the kinks in her back, and saw Socrates hovering near the window. At some point during the night, he had broken out of his cell. River glanced around and saw that her cell door was open. The others were as well.

"What are you doing?" she said, quietly slipping out of her cage. Socrates had his gaze fixed on something across the street, and he didn't speak. She went to his side and followed his gaze. Her jaw dropped as she saw the clockwork god sitting atop the front steps of the keep.

"You're not the only one who was busy last night," she said.

"I suspected the Keeper would want to bring the machine to the street for the sacrifice, and allow the townsfolk to see their god overlooking the proceedings. That is the reason he installed iron tracks in the castle floor. The Keeper could not do this during the day, with the citizens watching him. He waited until they slept, and then quietly pushed it out."

"I see steam," River said. "What is that thing?"

"It's called a steamscout. In the early days of the *Iron Horse,* steamscouts were sent out to map the terrain, to search for damaged tracks, and to lay new ones. They're like a smaller version of a locomotive. They have extremely powerful engines and, as you can see, arms to facilitate their work."

"Steamscouts did all this by themselves?" River said. "I thought you were the only automaton."

"You are correct. Steamscouts are not automatons. They have limited abilities. They cannot think or reason. Gyroscopes, weights, and other sensors tell the machine what to do. Because of this they were effective, but far from perfect. Steamscouts often required maintenance, and occasional rescuing."

"Where did this one come from?" said River. "The Keeper didn't find it in Sanctuary did he?"

"If he had, I would have known. I lived alone in the city for a thousand years. It is more likely that the Keeper's ancestors came across the steamscout in the wilderness. Perhaps they even found it here, at this castle."

"They didn't build the castle, then?"

"No. It is clear from the weathering of the stonework and timbers that these people neither built it, nor understand how to maintain it. Their ancestors simply happened upon it and staked their claim. You would be surprised how often this happens as cultures rise and fall throughout the ages."

River turned to face him, leaning back against the wall next to the window. "Socrates, what happened to these people? Why do their dead rise from the grave?"

"Starfall. Their well is tainted with it."

River's eyes widened. "For all these years, they've been drinking it?"

141

"I'm afraid so."

"But I don't understand. They seem so... *normal.*" She waved her hand, indicating the handful of peasants who had appeared in the street below. "When the people of Sanctuary were exposed to Starfall, they became Tal'mar and Kanters. The Starfall changed their bodies so they weren't human anymore."

"Those were heavily concentrated exposures," Socrates said. "These people ingest no more than a cup of Starfall in their entire lifetimes. It's not enough to affect physical manifestation, but the cumulative effects are enough to stimulate the motor cortex even after an individual dies."

"Cortex?"

"Yes, the part of the human brain that controls movement. You've seen the creatures they call Ancients. Think about what you observed: they act without reason or thought. They are motivated by some simple base instinct that attracts them to the living like the flame attracts the moth. They don't understand it, but some deep animalian part of their mind wishes to be alive again."

"That's horrible," River said. "How do you know all this?"

"I've seen it before," Socrates said.

"Where? In Sanctuary?"

"Yes. It was very, very long ago."

One by one, the other prisoners had awakened and come forward to listen to the conversation. Socrates now had an attentive audience of nine people staring at him. Shayla spoke up:

"Do you know how to stop these creatures?" she said.

"I can devise a filtration system for the well," Socrates said. "It will prevent this from happening in the future. But I think that is not what you mean. The only way to stop the undead corpses is to destroy their brains entirely. It would be best to burn them."

"But they won't go on like that forever," Shayla said. "Surely, the brains will eventually rot away to nothing."

"You would be surprised," Socrates said. "Starfall is energetic matter. In some cases, the Starfall can protect the section of brain that animates the body. As you have seen, some of these corpses still move even after most of the body has decayed away to nothing. Fire is the only sure way to end their suffering."

"But how can we burn them all?" said Kale. "There must be thousands of them."

"We have very little choice in the matter," Socrates said. "There are ways to attract the creatures. We could draw them into a trap and destroy them all at once -or most of them- but such plans mean nothing without the will of the people. You must remember, we're talking about their *Ancients*. Misguided as they may be, the townsfolk have worshiped these creatures for centuries. Such traditions do not pass away in one night."

"Then they'll be doomed," said River. "If they won't kill the Ancients, sooner or later the Ancients will kill them. It's already happening. Look at them. They're starving for fear of going into the forest!"

"Then I say we don't give them a choice," Kale said. "I say we kill the Keeper, and then trap all the

Ancients, just as you said. Once they're gone, the people will understand."

"Will they?" Socrates said loudly. "Do you think you can walk into their city and destroy their gods, and the townspeople will be grateful to you? Because that is what you have just described."

Kale slumped his shoulders and he sighed. "Maybe not," he said meekly, "but we have to do something."

"He's right," River said. "Socrates, even if we could escape and never look back, we can't just leave these people like this. We must do something for them."

Socrates stared at her a moment and then drew his gaze over the others. "Is this how the rest of you feel?"

"I'd like to help," Thane said. "But I think our safety is the first priority. We are in real danger here. I won't risk my life -or Shayla's- unnecessarily."

"Understood," said Socrates. "I'm relatively certain we can escape quite easily, but we must weigh the consequences of such actions. If we were to escape, we would put the crew of the *Iron Horse* in danger. Even if we made it safely to the train, we'd still have to fight our way out of the city. Casualties would be almost certain. So you see, there is no safe path before us."

"In that case," said Thane, "I suppose we should take the high road. I wouldn't want the blood of your crewmen on my conscience."

"Nor I," said Shayla. "I will do as you wish, Socrates."

"Very well. We will show the people a better way, but it will be up to them to follow. We can patiently and gently guide them to the truth, but if the citizens of Blackstone still reject it, we must leave them to their fate."

"How can we do that?" said River. "Tell us what to do."

Socrates turned his gaze to the street, and nodded in the direction of the steamscout-god. "We must expose the Keeper and his machine. And we must do this without intervening in any way."

"It's just a machine," said Kale. "Should be easy enough to break it. Then the people would understand what it is."

"You're not understanding me," said Socrates. "It is not enough to simply destroy the machine. It must *fail* on its own. The citizens must see it fail. We cannot risk touching it."

"That's impossible," Kale said, frowning.

"It would seem so. And yet I see no other course."

"I have an idea," said River. Their gazes shifted to her.

"Well?" said Kale. "What's your plan?"

"Thane, your shaving mirror," she said, grinning. "Give it to me."

Thane gave her a perplexed look as pulled the shaving kit out of the hidden compartment in his boot. He opened the leather case and produced the small metal mirror, and handed it to her. River accepted it and then pushed past Kale and the others, stepping up to the window. She held her arm out and tilted the mirror so that it caught the sunlight and reflected it across the street at the steamscout.

"Caution," Socrates said. "Setting fire to their god will not solve our problem, River."

"I'm not going to set it on fire," she said. "Just heating it up a little."

Socrates stared at her for a moment, and then his face lit up. A deep laugh rumbled out of his chest. "Well done, child. I see that you have been paying attention."

"I don't understand," said Kale. "What is she doing?"

"Sophisticated machines have certain sensors that enable their movement," Socrates explained. "One of those sensors is called a gyroscope. It's a fantastic creation. Without it, even I would not exist."

"Fantastic, but delicate," River said, grinning.

"Indeed," said Socrates. "The slightest bit of heat can bend a wire or metal plate and render it entirely useless. River is redirecting the sunlight in such a way that it will damage the steamscout's gyroscope."

Socrates leaned forward, narrowing his eyes. "Yes, that's it," he said. "Watch the strut riser. A bit lower... there! Now, hold it steady. It shouldn't take more than a minute or so."

The group pressed closer around them, each straining for a better view. One of the crewmen at the rear of the group tried to lean forward to see over Kale's shoulder. He lost his balance, knocking Kale forward. Kale stumbled into Thane who in turn bumped into River. She gasped as the mirror slipped from her grip. They all watched in horror as the mirror tumbled through the air and landed noisily on the street below. The instant it hit the ground, several peasants in the town square drew their gazes up to the window.

"There!" someone shouted. "The prisoners are escaping!"

There was a flurry of cloaks and rattling armor as the watchmen came racing to the tower. Socrates pulled away from the window and fixed the others with a hard stare.

"What fool did that?" he said angrily. They all shuffled nervously and avoided his gaze. Socrates shook his head. "Never mind. Back into your cages. Move!"

"But we could escape!" Kale said. "We could hold them off at the door!"

"For what?" said Socrates. "Have you already forgotten what I told you, fool?"

Kale turned and dejectedly walked back to his cage, shaking his head all the way, mumbling about not understanding the plan at all. Thane stepped in behind him and closed the door. River and the others followed suit, filing quickly into their cells and then, tragically, locking the doors behind them. A moment later, the commander of the watch and half a dozen fighters burst into the room, swords at the ready. As they realized the captives were all in their cages, they stopped short and stood there, confused.

"Which one of you tried to escape?" the commander said finally.

No one spoke.

"The doors are all locked," said one of the men. "It was a false alarm."

The commander eyed the group suspiciously. He turned to his second in command. "Put two watchmen in here for the rest of the day. If they try anything, sound the alarm."

"Yes, sir!"

Chapter 17

"I knew it would be something like this!" a muffled voice shouted in the railcar below Micah's room. "I knew Socrates would abandon us, or worse!"

Micah leaned closer to the floor, listening intently. Ever since his escape from the tower and return to the *Iron Horse,* he'd kept mostly to his personal space in the attic over the library car, especially since the train had arrived in Blackstone. Socrates had warned Micah what might happen to him if the Keeper and his men found him. Micah had no stomach for danger, and he had taken the warning to heart.

The attic was a large space filled mostly with Micah's maps and a collection of books he had been reading. The roof was only four feet tall in the middle, just big enough for him to walk around. He had a bookshelf pressed up against one wall and a small desk with a chair where he could read or work on his maps. The only other furnishing was his bed, which was nothing more than a feather mattress with a pillow and blanket. The room was lit by a single oil lantern that hung by a hook from the ceiling.

"Socrates didn't abandon us," another voice said in the room below. "He was arrested! We all saw it."

"Fine, whatever. It all adds up the same. What'd he leave us with? The Keeper's guards beatin' down the doors, that's what!"

"I say we fight 'em off. We've got muskets."

"And then what?" said the first man. "Are we gonna fight our way through the whole city, riskin' our necks just to rescue that machine?"

"Socrates ain't just a machine."

"Oh, come on! He's made a' gears and springs just like a windup toy. You've all seen it. He don't think or feel. Not like us."

"You don't know that."

"Sure I do. What machine can *feel,* Ned? I'll tell you what: None! And the fact that he brought us here is proof. What do you think he expected to happen? He wasn't thinkin' like a man. He was doin' what a machine does!"

"We gotta do somethin'," a third voice chimed in. "That door ain't gonna hold long."

"Leave it to me," said the first. "I'll work it out."

"Yeah? How you gonna do that?"

"I'm gonna make a *deal,* boys."

"I don't like this," the third voice said.

"Well, what's it gonna be then? You with us or against us? I'll turn you over to the Keeper right now, if you like."

"No, I don't want that."

"Good. Then we're all in agreement. Just follow along with me and keep yer mouths shut."

There was a lot of shuffling and Micah heard the group move toward the front of the train. "It's all right!" the first man shouted, his voice muffled in the distance. "We're comin' out!"

Micah crept noiselessly across the attic, and cautiously pulled back the corner of the curtain over one of the narrow floor-level windows. He saw the crew disembarking from the front of the train with their hands held high. The guards lined them up along the car, and then the commander sent men inside to search the train. Micah saw the commander and Burk speaking in hushed tones, but couldn't make out a single word.

The sound of movement and voices wafted up from below as the guards walked up and down the train cars. They hurriedly finished their search and returned to the commander with no extra prisoners. Micah was sure they hadn't searched the entire train because it stretched more than half a mile into the distance, and they had performed their search in a matter of minutes. The commander must have observed this as well, because as soon as they had returned, he loudly ordered them back onto the train to finish the job.

"And this time do it right!" he shouted after them.

Micah stole a worried glance at the tower, but saw only darkness beyond the window. Kale and River were locked in there, along with Socrates and the others. It occurred to him that perhaps he'd be safer in the tower with them, but Micah didn't dare move for fear of the guards below.

He heard them moving slowly through the cars, searching more thoroughly this time. He glanced at the trap door in the floor at the end of the room and caught his breath. He'd never bothered to latch it! Micah turned away from the window and scurried towards the door. As he did, he heard the unmistakable sound of a guard searching the car beneath him. Micah froze, listening intently.

"This one's clear," the guard shouted. "Keep going."

"What about that?" said another voice.

"There's nothing up there."

"Yeah? Fine, you tell the commander then."

"Oh, all right. Give me a minute."

Micah cringed as he heard the sound of the guard climbing up the ladder. In a panic, he realized he couldn't possibly make it to the latch in time. Micah glanced around the attic, looking for a place to hide. The mattress wouldn't work, it was too obvious. The bookshelf was wedged up tight against the wall...

Micah scurried across the floor and squeezed himself into the narrow space under the desk. He twisted sideways, trying to conceal himself in the shadows, but couldn't quite seem to fit. He heard the sound of the trap door opening behind him, but couldn't see it from his position. A ray of light fell across the floor. Micah nearly squealed as the light fell on his exposed right arm. He awkwardly grabbed his arm with his left hand and pulled. With a painful yank, he managed to get his arm out of the light. He grimaced, struggling not to breathe as the guard stuck his head into the attic. Micah could hear the man's heavy breathing. He could all but feel the man's eyes on him.

Micah's heart pounded in his ears and his lungs burned for a breath of air, but he clenched his jaw and pressed his lips firmly together. He closed his eyes. *Maps,* he thought. *Think of maps!* He visualized a mountain in the distance, and a river winding through the foothills. He imagined the quill strokes across the parchment, the arrangement of lines and shadow as the image slowly came to life...

At last, Micah could hold his breath no more. He released his grip on his arm, allowing his chest to expand, and sucked in a deep gasp. At that exact moment, the door slammed shut and the guard dropped back down to the floor. Micah's heart hammered in his chest as he realized how much noise he had just made. Micah listened intently, his eyes wild, his chest heaving and falling. Had the guard heard him? In the room below, the guard mumbled something and then went quiet. For the life of him, Micah couldn't tell if the guard had left, or if the man was simply waiting to spring back into the attic and catch him by surprise.

Seconds ticked by. At last, Micah heard voices coming from the next car. He sighed as he realized that one of them was the same guard. It had to be, because he knew for a fact that there were only two men on the train. A moan escaped his lips as he awkwardly twisted out of the small space. Spasms shot up and down his back, and Micah lay back on the floor, waiting for the pain to subside, praying to the ghosts of his ancestors and thanking them for his escape.

When at last he could move, Micah crawled back to the window. The *Horse's* crew had been moved, probably inside the keep. Only a few peasants remained on the street. He caught a glint of light in the corner of his eye and glanced back toward the tower where his friends had been imprisoned. He saw River leaning out of the tower window with Thane's shaving mirror in her hand.

153

"What the devils?" he mumbled, watching her move the mirror back and forth. The light flashed in his eyes and then flitted away. He craned his neck, trying to get a glimpse of what she might be aiming at, and realized it was on the other side of the train. Slowly, Micah crawled back across the attic and peeked out the window. There, for the first time, he saw the clockwork god resting atop the stairs. He noticed the beam of light tracking back and forth over the front of the machine, and frowned. For the life of him, Micah couldn't fathom what River was up to.

Micah wasn't familiar with machinery, and therefore knew nothing about gears and gyroscopes. What he could guess was that River was trying to make something happen to the machine. She wanted it to start, or to stop, or possibly just to catch fire. He couldn't imagine which, but he knew it had to be one of these things, and knowing River, there must be a sound plan behind it. Micah crawled back across the train and peeked back up at her, just in time to see the mirror slip from River's hand. He saw the peasants cry out, and watched the guards go racing into the tower. He held his breath for the next few moments, fearing something terrible was about to happen. River disappeared from the window and everything went quiet.

At last, the guards filed back out of the tower. They locked the door and disappeared into the keep. Up above, everything in the window was dark and quiet. Apparently, his companions were now locked back in their cages. Micah drew his gaze back to the street and saw the tiny silver mirror lying there, glinting in the morning sunlight.

"I see how it is now," he grumbled, casting a glance back at the darkened tower window. "I've got to save the lot of you."

Chapter 18

Commander Toolume watched from the keep as his guards cleared the train and brought the prisoners into the main hall. A few steps back, the Keeper paced back and forth in front of his desk, wringing his hands, pausing now and then to sip from a goblet of wine.

"They're all inside," the Commander said. "What do you want me to do?"

The Keeper paused to finish off his wine. He gulped it down and then stared into the empty goblet. "I should have you kill them all," he said. "We'd be better off getting rid of them."

"We can't do that," the commander said.

"Oh? Perhaps you've forgotten who's running this town."

The commander clenched his jaw and took a deep breath. "We both know very well that you're in charge. The problem is that soon there won't be a town left to run. We are dying, cousin. We need new blood. These strangers... they make not be *like* us, but they will learn. Once they see their leader destroyed and the power of our god, they will do whatever we say."

"If only it were that easy," the Keeper said. "The problem is that these men have seen the world. They know what's out there, and they understand things... If we let them in, it will only be a matter of time before they start telling stories and convincing the others to leave. Then what will we do?"

The commander leaned against the wall and folded his arms over his chest. "As you say, we could kill them. If we do that, we'll have to find a way to explain it to your subjects. The townsfolk will overlook the sacrifice. That's reasonable. But shedding innocent blood? They may not stand for that."

The Keeper cleared his throat as he poured another glass. "It seems you've put a great deal of thought into this matter. What do you suggest then, cousin?"

"You already know what I think. We should integrate them into the town. Marry them off to some of the widows. God knows we have dozens of them."

The Keeper settled into his desk and leaned forward, placing his head in his hands. He sighed deeply and then leaned back, staring at his companion.

"All right, then. We'll be hospitable, at least for now. Get them settled. Let them know how it is. If this fails, I will hold you personally accountable."

If it fails, it won't matter, the commander thought. He left the room and hurried downstairs. In the main hall of the keep, he located the crew of the *Iron Horse*. A dozen guards armed with spears and swords had lined them up against the back wall. He walked the line in front of them, eyeing them up and down, searching his mind for the words he needed. Was it possible to tell a man he was a captive and could never leave, and yet make it sound appealing?

Focus on the possibilities, he thought. *Offer them ale, gold, sex... whatever a man might want. Just offer it, even if we don't have it...* As he looked them over, one of the men spoke up. He was a muscular, bearded man with a dangerous glint in his eyes:

"What're you gonna do with us?" Burk demanded.

The commander looked him over. "Who are you?"

Burk stepped forward, flexing his massive muscles. "I'm the one you're talking to."

A slight smile turned up the corners of the commander's mouth. "You're the leader, then?"

"I am now. My name is Burk."

The commander turned to the guards. "Take the crew to the old Inn and give them rooms. They are not to leave until I say so." He turned his attention back to Burk and smiled. "All right then, let's you and I take a walk..."

Burk followed the commander out of the keep and down the main street. He observed the townsfolk going about their labors all around him. The women were all either old or malnourished. There weren't many men; none who could put up a fight anyway. Those that could had no doubt been recruited into the guard. At last, the commander spoke:

"What are you, a carpenter? A smith, perhaps?"

Burk nodded at that.

"I see. And how did you come to be the leader of this crew?"

"You might say there was an opening," Burk said with a toothy grin. "Seems our old leader got himself in a pickle."

"Indeed. And you didn't waste a second, did you? You strike me as a man of opportunity, Burk. You could have wasted your energy trying to rally a defense, trying to save your leader. Instead you chose to betray him." He paused in the middle of the street and they stood there facing one another.

"You tryin' to say somethin'?"

"Yes. I'm saying that I have use for a man of your *skills*."

"Ah, that's what it is then. Lookin' for some opportunity yerself, ain't ya? Ya got a problem with the Keeper?"

The commander's smile vanished. "This conversation is between the two of us. If any word of this ever comes to light, I'll have you skinned alive and hang you over the wall until the Ancients rip you apart, piece by piece. Do you understand?"

"I think I do."

"Good. Tell your men to make themselves comfortable. They may choose women and homes, but they must stay inside the wall. As long as they abide by our rules, they will be well cared for. They will have food, drink, and so on."

"That's mighty generous of you, Commander. And what is it you expect from us, in return?"

"When the time comes, I will call on you. It's time for a change of leadership in this town, and it's coming soon. Will you be ready?"

"I'm always ready," Burk said.

The commander turned away with a grim smile on his face. *That one's dangerous,* he thought. *I'll have to kill him soon.*

Chapter 19

Socrates had made it clear that none of the group should attempt to escape. Not yet, anyway. He was determined to see the plan through to the end. Unfortunately, the details of the plan were still elusive and River's nerves were growing more frayed by the minute. Through hand signs and whispers, she tried to communicate to Socrates that she wasn't sure if she'd succeeded in damaging the steamscout. River had managed to hit the gyroscope with sunlight reflected on Thane's shaving mirror, but not for very long, and she had no way to be sure if that had been enough. If forced to guess, she'd have said it wasn't. She tried to explain this to Socrates, but he just stared at her, his gold-flecked deep brown simian eyes glaring back at her under those heavy brows.

River was starting to wonder if Burk's arguments about the mechanical gorilla were correct. Maybe Socrates really couldn't feel. Maybe he really didn't understand what it meant to be human. If that was true, then where did that leave the crew? If Socrates was incapable of feeling something as simple and primal as *fear*, then how could he truly understand the danger they were in? And how could he act appropriately?

The rest of the afternoon passed in miserable, agonizing silence. Any attempt at conversation made by River and her companions, the guards quickly silenced with threats of violence, or worse. This didn't frighten River because she knew she had nothing to fear from two guards who could be easily overwhelmed. It was the waiting -and worrying- that she couldn't stand.

Later, as the shadows were lengthening across the stone floor and the townsfolk began gathering in the street below the tower to make preparations for the execution, a clicking noise by the window caught River's attention. She was half-asleep, having long since given up on her attempts to communicate with Socrates. She was sitting in the corner of her cage with her back up against he bars, her eyes closed. Half-remembered images of the mother she barely knew were fleeting through her mind. The sound snapped River out of her daydreams and she sat upright, scanning the room. She heard the noise again and fixed her gaze on the window. Micah's face appeared briefly, and then disappeared. River's eyes widened. She glanced at the guards and realized they had settled down on chairs by the door. Their eyes were closed, but she couldn't tell if they were asleep or just resting. Quietly, she pushed to her feet and went to the front of her cage.

Micah appeared again. He nervously glanced around the room and then smiled as he met her gaze. River shook her head and mouthed the words: *What are you doing!* Micah fumbled in his pocket for a moment and then produced the mirror. He had retrieved it from the street below. He held it up so she could see it, and River's face lit up. She glanced at the guards and then at Socrates, wondering if she could attract the ape's attention without waking their captors.

Socrates had turned to face the wall after ignore-ing her for the larger part of the day. Now, with his back bent to her, she couldn't even tell if the creature was awake. River wasn't even sure if the gorilla needed to sleep. He was a machine after all, but Socrates also had so many human traits. She'd seen him eat and drink, read books, and even cook. Was Socrates human enough that he required sleep? River made a mental note to ask him later, if they survived.

Cautiously, she bent low and rapped her knuckled on the stone floor. Socrates didn't stir, but one of the guards did. He twisted in his chair, and shuffled his feet. River grimaced as she watched him. The guard sighed. He readjusted himself slightly, and then went right back to sleep. River pressed her face close to the bars and very quietly whispered in Socrates' direction:

"Psst!"

Socrates didn't move.

River threw her gaze back to Micah. She shrugged, indicating that she didn't know what to do. Micah rolled his eyes and sagged his shoulders. He placed the mirror gently on the windowsill and started to climb through. River winced as Micah pushed up onto his belly and swung his legs over. The fabric of his breeches grazed the mirror ever so slightly, and it jumped sideways. River's stomach lurched. She waved her arms, trying to get the small man's attention, but he was oblivious.

With a considerable amount of rustling, Micah got himself turned around and then lowered himself to the floor. On the way down, his vest caught on the windowsill and he very nearly got himself stuck. He heaved himself back far enough to loosen the fabric, and at last his boots touched the floor. Surprisingly, the mirror still rested on the edge of the windowsill. River took a deep breath and willed her pounding heart to slow down. Micah snatched up the mirror and hurried over to her cage.

"Thought you might need this," he whispered with a wink.

River accepted it gratefully. "I do, but..." she gestured at the lock on her cage. She glanced out the window and saw the sunlight quickly waning. Now that she had the mirror, River might actually be able to finish the task of disabling the steamscout. Unfortunately, she only had minutes to do it, and she had no way to open the lock. She considered trying to explain their plan and the workings of the steamscout to Micah, but quickly banished the idea. Micah was a kind and gentle man, but utterly useless when it came to things mechanical.

River glanced at Socrates and made another *"Psst!"* sound. At last, he stirred. Socrates turned to face them and Micah rushed over to his cage. He whispered something inaudible and waved in River's direction. Socrates followed Micah's gaze, and River held up the mirror. She made a frantic hand motion, pleading for the ape to hurry up and unlock the cages. Socrates stared at her for a moment, seemingly lost in deep thought. He lowered his gaze to Micah and in a low voice, said, "I'm sorry, my friend."

Then Socrates glanced at the guards and in a raspy voice shouted: "RUN, MICAH!"

The shout instantly woke the guards. One of them flinched so wildly that he fell backwards in his chair and crashed to the floor. The second guard leapt to his feet and dropped the sword that had been resting across his knees. It clattered loudly across the stones. By this time, the rest of the prisoners were wide awake. They all joined in, shouting, "Run, Micah! Get out of here! RUN!"

Micah's initial response was to freeze. A shiver of terror crawled down his spine as he realized that his friend and commander had betrayed him. Then, as the others joined in on the shouting, the words somehow worked their way into Micah's brain and it slowly dawned on him that he *really did* have to get out of there. He turned, sprinting for the window as the guards struggled to get to their feet.

Micah had never run so fast in his life. He took three steps and launched himself at the window. He somehow made a slight miscalculation and managed to fling himself right through the opening. Micah was half a heartbeat away from flying over the edge of the tower and plunging to his death. He thrust his arms out, flailing wildly for a handhold. Somehow, he just barely managed to catch the edge of the window frame. As he latched onto it, Micah's momentum sent him spinning through the opening. He twisted around, slammed into the outside wall, and lost his grip. Micah dropped out of sight, and Shayla screamed as he disappeared.

For a moment, Micah thought it was all over. Then, as he fell, one of his hands miraculously closed on the ledge below the window. His fingers latched onto the narrow stone precipice, and by the sheerest luck, he managed to hang on. For a few seconds, Micah just dangled there, shaking, trying to breathe. Then he heard voices coming from the window above, and the sound spurred him to action.

Micah's legs flailed wildly as he began pulling himself up. The sharp stone corners of the ledge bit into his palms, but Micah forced himself to keep climbing. He twisted, bringing a leg around to place one foot precariously on the ledge. Overhead, the sounds of shouting drifted out of the tower. The guards appeared at the window and they stood there a moment, staring down at him. With a grunt, Micah heaved himself the rest of the way over the ledge and somehow managed to stand up with his face pressed against the wall. Even twisted sideways, Micah barely fit in the narrow space. Over his head, he heard a voice shout:

"There! I'm goin' after him!"

"I'll go around," the second guard replied.

Micah craned his neck around to catch a glimpse of the first guard climbing out of the window. Micah was out of reach, but not for long. He had to move. He threw his arms out to the sides, balancing his weight awkwardly against the wall as he took his first step. He wavered a moment, and then managed to bring his second foot forward. A few steps behind him, the guard grunted as he lowered himself down to the ledge.

"Hey! Get back here!" the guard shouted. This only spurred Micah forward. He put on a burst of speed, hurrying along the ledge as fast as he dared. A gust of wind hit the wall and for a moment, Micah thought it might push him right off. He leaned forward, pressing his cheek against the cold stone, and grimaced as the wind battered at him. Two yards away, the guard lunged for him.

Micah stepped aside, plunging dangerously forward as he sought to escape his attacker. Just a few yards ahead, he saw the corner where the tower met the battlements. Rather than struggling to maintain his precarious balance, Micah leapt from his perch, legs braced, arms flailing wildly. He landed on the very edge of the wall, balanced on his toes. For a brief moment, Micah was at the mercy of fate. One gust of wind might either push him to safety, or send him plummeting to his death.

Micah tilted his head forward, trying to move his balance towards the keep. He felt his weight shift slightly. With a terrified *squeal*, Micah leapt through the battlements and touched down safely on the keep's lookout. He threw a glance over his shoulder and saw the grim-faced soldier glaring at him as the man took another unsteady step. That was enough to prompt him forward.

Micah hurried across the walkway and climbed the opposite parapet, thinking he'd make towards the trees as he had before. Unfortunately, he suddenly realized this would bring him within arm's reach of the guard. Instead, he clambered easily onto the low, sloping roof of the keep, and hurriedly began climbing towards the peak. Behind him, the door at the end of the walkway swung open and the second guard appeared, brandishing his sword.

"Get back here, sewer rat!" he shouted.

"Go after him!" shouted the first. "He's got nowhere to go!"

Micah reached the peak of the roof and stood there a moment, watching the guards struggle to climb onto the roof below. As they did, half a dozen more came racing out of the keep and onto the

167

walkway. One of them had a loaded crossbow, which he leveled in Micah's direction and fired.

Micah flung himself to his belly as the crossbow bolt whizzed over his head. Frantically, he rolled over the peak and pushed to his feet on the opposite side. Micah bolted across the roof toward the north-western corner, and came to a screeching halt as he saw the world drop away at the edge of the castle. His stomach lurched as he gazed at the sheer drop, hundreds of feet down into a stony ravine.

He threw a wild glance back and forth, looking for some route of escape. There were no ramparts here; no walkway or outthrust ledges onto which he might climb. There was nothing but a straight drop into that abyss of sharp stone and hard, barren earth. Micah turned back, staring at the peak of the roof as he heard the guards clambering up the opposite side, and raised his arms in the air.

"I surrender!" he shouted hopelessly. "Don't shoot!"

Chapter 20

As Micah was fleeing for his life, back inside the tower Socrates waited for the second guard to leave the room and then quickly retrieved his lock-picking tool from the container in his torso. Within seconds, he had the door to his cell open. He rushed over to River's cell and held out his hand.

"Give me the mirror!" he commanded.

River glared at him. "Why?" she said. "You handed Micah over to them! How can I trust you?"

"I did what I must," Socrates said. "Believe me, it brought me no pleasure."

"He's right," Thane said from his cell. "It was the only way. Now we have the time to finish the task, but only if we hurry!"

River looked Thane up and down and then brought her gaze back to Socrates. She saw impatience in his face, and frustration, but not anger. In fact, if she hadn't known better, River might have even thought it was despair that she saw in his eyes. She still didn't know what to think of the simian. She didn't know if she believed he could feel emotions or not. If not, he could put on a pretty convincing show.

Grudgingly, she handed the mirror over. Socrates accepted it, and raced to the window. He glanced around to be sure no one would see him, and then extended his arm out into the sunlight. River saw the light glinting off the polished silver surface, and the whole world seemed to stop. The clouds hanging over the horizon were pink and orange, hues that somehow seemed more like an omen of fire and blood than the splendor of a brilliant sunset. Already, the sky in the distance was growing dark.

River heard the sounds of the guards shouting across the battlements as they pursued Micah onto the roof, and a thousand worries flashed through her mind. Would Micah escape? If not, what would the guards do to him? How long would it be before they returned? How long would it be before someone saw the massive midnight-blue gorilla leaning out the stockade window with a mirror in his hand?

River started pacing, her senses alert, her frantic mind ticking off the seconds. How long until the sun set? Was there even enough daylight left to complete the task? Forty seconds passed. River continued to pace, her nerves raw with tension. Around her, the others came to life. Kale and Thane pressed their faces to the iron bars, their eyes fixed on Socrates. Shayla frowned, worrying her long auburn hair into knots around her finger. Sixty seconds. Ninety...

More than two minutes passed before Socrates finally lowered the mirror with a grim look on his face. He hurried back to his cell, pausing on the way to reach into Thane's cage and return the bard his mirror.

"Thank you," Socrates said.

"My pleasure," Thane said with a bow. He held the mirror up, examining it. "A few small scratches, but no worse for wear. A small price to pay, if it worked." He gazed into Socrates' face. "Did it work?"

Socrates leapt back into his cage, slammed the door shut, and settled down on the straw pile without a word. Seconds later, the guards returned carrying Micah between two of them. The diminutive fellow shot Socrates a foul look as the guards locked him in a cage and this time, shackled his wrists. Unable to explain the situation in front of the guards, Socrates sighed and then turned around to face the wall again.

*

An hour later, Commander Toolume returned to the tower. He was accompanied by a dozen well-armed fighters. "Escort the prisoners to the square," he ordered the men. "Chain them to the pyre. *Do not* give them a chance to escape. Especially that one," he added, pointing at Micah. Micah glared at Socrates, who still had his back turned. They hadn't exchanged a single word since Micah's return. In fact, Socrates hadn't spoken to anyone.

As the guards escorted their prisoners out of the tower, the captives got their first glimpse of the pyre. The townsfolk had erected tall posts in the middle of the street not far from the square. They had outfitted each post with chains and shackles. For good measure, they had also installed iron hooks in the street to secure the prisoners' chains. The pyre itself was rather unimpressive: a stack of tree branches and rotting, discarded lumber that surrounded the posts.

"Doesn't look like much," Kale grumbled as they approached the scene.

"Looks dry enough to burn," Thane said in a grim voice. "Is that kerosene I smell?"

Kale scanned the wood pile and grimaced as he saw the telltale discoloration where the executioners had indeed poured kerosene over the wood. In one spot, he noted a shiny patch of cobblestone where the oil had dripped down and formed into a puddle. He cast a worried glance at Socrates.

Socrates was in the center of the group, preceded by Kale and River, and followed by the rest of the prisoners. Micah was at the far end. In this order, the guards lined them up in front of the posts and secured their shackles. Around them, the townsfolk continued piling bundles of sticks and branches onto the pyre. They completed this task as twilight deepened, and the pyre had grown large enough that it could easily consume the entire group.

"They just keep coming," Micah observed at some point. "Where are they finding all this wood?"

"They'll miss it, come winter," River said, loud enough that those nearby could hear her quite clearly. Then she added, "That is, those who haven't already starved to death." A peasant woman glanced at her as she dropped a bundle of sticks onto the pyre and then averted her gaze. No one, it seemed, would look them in the eyes. Not even the guards.

"They know what they're doing is wrong," Micah said. "I can see their guilt."

"Aye, little one," Shayla said. "I see it as well. Though it does not seem to be stopping them."

As darkness fell over the land and the full moon began its slow ascent into the sky, the guards brought a podium on the back of a flatbed wagon and maneuvered it into place in front of the pyre.

"Don't care much for the looks of that," Micah noted as the townsfolk started gathering in the square carrying torches.

"Handy, having all those torches around," Kale muttered. "Much better than rubbing sticks together."

"Very funny," said River. "Just our luck they'll drop one and set the whole thing ablaze on accident."

"I don't like any of it," said one of the crewmen. Another added, "I wish they'd just kill me and get it over with."

"Isn't that Burk?" River said, gazing across the crowd of onlookers. Kale followed her gaze, squinting.

"I think it is! What is he doing?"

"He's drinking a tankard of ale," Socrates said. "And holding a woman in his arm."

"Doesn't seem too broken up about all this, does he?" Kale muttered.

"He turned on you the minute you were arrested," Micah said. "I saw the whole thing. He couldn't wait to make a deal with the Keeper."

They fell silent, their angry stares fixed on the blacksmith. After a few minutes, Burk disappeared into the crowd. River spoke up:

"Socrates, last night you said you'd seen creatures like the Ancients before?"

"I have," Socrates said. "In Sanctuary."

"I don't understand. I thought Sanctuary was abandoned after the Starfall poisoned their water supply."

"It was, eventually. At the beginning, no one knew about Starfall. We understood its powers to generate energy, but we didn't know the effects it could have on human flesh. Like the people of this town, we learned those lessons the hard way."

"What does this mean?" said Shayla. "What is this *Sanctuary* city you speak of?"

"It's a city in the northern Wastelands," Kale said. "Our ancestors came from there. The humans, the Tal'mar, even the giants all descended from that same race of people."

"They were all human until the Starfall poisoned their water," River said. "It changed them, apparently in more ways than we knew. Tell us what happened there, Socrates."

The mechanical beast let out a strangely human sigh. He closed his eyes, the gears inside his body whirring as he searched his memory banks. "Our people were already at war when it happened. It began with two brothers, the sons of an old toymaker. The man was a widower. Despite this, he raised his children the best he could, showering them with love and gifts, withholding from them nothing. In his heart, the poor old man believed perhaps he could compensate for the loss of their mother in this way.

"Even at a young age, it was apparent that the boys were very different from each other. The youngest took after his father, learning to make toys and planning to take over his father's business someday. He specialized in robotic inventions that looked like animals and small children. They were wildly popular, and this made the family a great deal of money.

"Meanwhile, the elder brother made toys as well, but from the very beginning they were different. The eldest boy made toy soldiers armed with weapons, and war machines. He created vast armies of these tiny robots and enacted miniature battles in the city parks. People came from all over the city to watch and cheer as the robots destroyed one another. It was all fun and exciting for them you see, but these things were all portents of things to come. In time, the boys became men, and they turned their passion for engineering into greater things. The younger brother developed his robots so that they could serve the city. He designed them to repair buildings and machines, to clean the streets, even to build more of themselves. It was truly incredible, what he accomplished.

"While this was all going on, the elder brother took an interest in the politics of the city. He fell in with a fringe group known as *Clockwork Axis*. The leaders of this group believed in overthrowing the government to create a monarchy. They believed the people of Sanctuary were lazy and corrupt, and that their lives would be better managed by men of superior intellect."

"Meaning the Axis," River said.

"Of course. Men don't overthrow governments just to create a vacuum. They do it to acquire power."

"What happened next?"

"The older brother tried to convince the people of his beliefs. He ran for the city council and lost. The press made a mockery of him, and this infuriated him. The Axis withdrew into the tunnels under the city, where they quietly gained power and influence. In the meanwhile, the toy soldiers and war machines the elder brother had designed evolved.

He reengineered his ideas into highly sophisticated weapons. Then, when the time was right, his clockwork army struck.

"They attacked in the night with flying machines armed with bombs. The soldiers marched into the streets, corralling people like animals and locking them in special buildings designated as detention areas. It was all out war, and the city was not prepared for it. Perhaps, in a way, the boy had been right. A more proactive leadership would have expected such an eventuality and been ready for it. When it was over, those few who survived came to call it the *Clockwork War*."

"What about the Ancients?" said Micah. "How did that happen?"

"I was just getting to that. During the attacks, one of the bombs struck perilously close to a storage facility. A small container of Starfall exploded, destroying a large part of the city and setting loose tens of thousands of gallons of Starfall. The liquid seeped into the waterways and aquifers, poisoning the entire food supply."

"Even as their bodies were being contaminated, the people were tortured and executed by the clockwork soldiers. The elder brother finally realized the full horror of what he had done when he saw the corpse of his own sibling lurching through the city streets. He had already gone mad at this point, driven insane by his lust for power. The image of his little brother's undead corpse simply drove him over the edge. In his rage, he set out to destroy the city and everyone living in it. Were his days not cut short, he would have killed everyone."

"Cut short?" said Kale. "What happened to him?"

Socrates locked gazes with Kale. "I killed him."

Commander Toolume appeared in the square. He climbed onto the wagon and raised his arms high. A murmur went up in the crowd, and some began to cheer and whistle.

"Quiet, everyone!" the commander shouted. "It is time for the ceremony to begin." The townsfolk cheered as the commander stepped to the side, and the Keeper climbed up next to him.

"Ladies and gentlemen, the prisoners before you stand accused of the worst kind of sacrilege. We are an open and forthright people, but when we invited these strangers into our town they turned against us like vipers. They have disregarded our customs and broken our laws. Worst of all, they have committed sacrilege against our ancestors and our god. Let there be no doubt that we are an honest and just people. On this night, justice shall be done!"

The crowd roared with approval and the Keeper cast a wicked glance over his shoulder at the prisoners. When the noise had died down a bit, he continued:

"Let us hasten now towards resolution. Commander, ready your men to light the pyre. I will waken our sleeping god, so that he may look upon his judgment with satisfaction."

The crowd cheered as the Keeper climbed off the wagon and made his way across the square to the front of the keep. His black and red robes melted into the shadows there, but even from that distance, River heard the squeaking noise of a door opening as the Keeper crawled inside the steamscout. She rolled her eyes.

"How can they not understand what he's doing?" she said. "Why can't they see?"

Socrates twisted his head to stare at her. "They see what they choose," he said. "Or rather, they *don't see* what they choose not to. Men are fickle creatures. They will happily believe a lie that promises what they want, rather than see a truth that doesn't."

"Who can live like that?" River said. "You can't fix anything if you won't even admit something's wrong."

"It's tempting to blame ignorance," said Socrates, "to believe they don't know any better. But when a wrong is committed and men turn away, it is most often not out of ignorance but pride. Of all mankind's emotions, it is pride that most often leads to their downfall."

"What about you?" said River. "Do you have emotions, Socrates? Do you feel?"

He raised his gaze to the distant stars. "Sometimes."

"And what about the rest of the time?"

"I try not to. But it usually doesn't work." He drew his gaze back to meet hers. "Have I disappointed you?"

"No... I know exactly what you mean. I try not to let my emotions get in the way, but they always seem to get the better of me. Sometimes, I think it would be nice not to feel."

"You mean like Burk over there?" Kale said, snarling. "Even Socrates is more human than him. When we get out of here-"

"Leave him be," Socrates said. "When it's time to deal with Burk, I'll handle it."

"Are you sure?" said Kale. "I've sliced bigger men than him in two."

Socrates shook his head. "We won't deal with our problems like that. Leave it to me. My train, my rules."

Kale sighed but didn't argue further.

At that moment, the steamscout's lights came on, illumining the crowd in the square. They gasped and cheered as the clockwork god was roused from its sleep. River heard the familiar sounds of clicking gears and whirring springs, and she shook her head.

"My good people, I have awakened!" the Keeper's voice announced from inside the steamscout. "I have risen from my sleep to see justice done!"

The crowd roared, and the commander silently ordered his men to bring their torches to the pyre. River gave Socrates a worried look, but the gorilla's eyes were fixed on the clockwork god.

"At my command," the Keeper shouted, raising one of the steamscout's arms. As it moved, something happened inside the machine. River distinctly heard the sound of grinding gears, followed by a loud whirring noise. At the same time, the steamscout's second arm dropped. It hit the stairs with a crash and continued to push, shaking as it lifted the machine sideways into the air.

Gasps and fearful shouts went up from the crowd as the whirring sound rose in pitch. The entire machine began shaking out of control, and the sound of grinding metal became almost intolerable. The steamscout lurched towards the stairs, and the crowd scattered fearfully. As their panic spread, the terrified citizens began to stampede out of the square. The guards saw the crowd rushing towards them and broke ranks. They threw their torches to the ground and ran down the street, fleeing from their furious god.

Across the square, the clockwork god tumbled forward. It rolled awkwardly down the stairs, clanging and banging all the way to the street. As it came to rest, the boiler overflowed, releasing the built up steam pressure with a loud *hissing* sound. Clouds of vapor rolled into the air. Inside the machine, the Keeper let out a scream.

"It worked," River said excitedly. "Socrates, it worked!"

"Too well, I'm afraid," he said, glancing at the pyre behind them. River craned her neck around and gasped as she saw flames licking up behind her. One of the discarded torches had fallen too close to the dry branches, and had set the pyre alight. The flames were already climbing quickly up the stacked branches.

"Wait!" River called out at the people racing by. "Stop! We'll be burned alive."

"Don't get your hopes up," Thane said bitterly. "That is what they came here to see."

River bit her lip. She bent forward, struggling against her bonds, but they held fast. Socrates flexed his massive biceps and pulled against the chains. The heavy posts bent slightly inward, but a few yards down Micah let out a yelp.

"Stop!" he shouted. "You're going to rip my arms off!"

Socrates released the pressure. He grimaced and shook his head. "It's no good. I can't pull these down without hurting someone."

"Then hurt him!" Kale said. "Better a broken arm than all of us burned alive!"

Socrates considered his options carefully as he watched the flames lick ever closer. Based on his calculations, he had approximately one minute to act before the fire reached them. His choices were limited. The only way he could break the chains was to risk injuring one of his companions. Sadly, Micah was at the end of the line where pressure would be the greatest. He was also the smallest of the group, and therefore the most likely to be harmed. Socrates was relatively sure Micah would sustain permanent damage.

What other choice did he have? Socrates didn't want to hurt even one of his companions, but wasn't the safety of the many more important than the well-being of just one? A frustrated roar erupted from his chest and a few yards away, Micah let out a horrified scream.

Chapter 21

Commander Toolume appeared before them. In his hand, he held the large metal ring with the key to their shackles.

"Let us go!" Shayla shouted. "Devils, get us out of here!"

The commander glanced over the group and then fixed his gaze on Socrates. "Before I let you go, promise me one thing: You won't hold me or my people accountable for the Keeper's actions."

"Done," Socrates said. He threw his head back and forth so the others could hear him. "No action is to be taken against the people of this town!"

"Agreed," said Thane.

"Sure, whatever," Kale said. "Get us out of here!"

The commander leapt into action. He started by releasing River and Socrates, who were closest to the flames. He moved his way up and down the line, unlocking their shackles as quickly as he could manage. As he freed them, the captives leapt away from the flames and gathered in the safety of the square a few yards back, where the air was fresh and cool and the well conveniently accessible.

In less than a minute, Commander Toolume had released the entire group. As they stood watching, the pyre erupted into a massive inferno, engulfing the posts where their shackles still hung suspended in the air.

"That could've been us," Micah said, gulping loudly.

"We wouldn't be the first," Thane said ominously. "These people have been handling their problems this way for a long time."

They heard a scream and hurried around the flames just in time to see the Keeper struggling to get out of the collapsed steamscout. Clouds of steam floated around him and occasional sparks lit up his face. The commander hurried over to help his cousin, and the rest of the group followed. The Keeper fell over and sprawled out across the ground. He lay there panting as the group arrived. He glanced up at them, and then averted his eyes shamefully.

"Help me up," he said, reaching for the commander. "Get me into the keep!"

The commander glared down at him with a baleful stare. "You have some explaining to do, Blaise."

"Do you forget who you're talking to?" the Keeper shouted. "I'm the Keeper of the Word! I am the prophet of god!"

"This god?" the commander said, kicking the steamscout. A broken gear came tumbling out and clattered to the ground. "I've put up with your arrogance and your intrigues for all my life, Blaise Toolume. I'm done with it. Guards!"

Two guards who had been hovering near the entrance of the keep came rushing forward. "Commander?" one of them said.

"Escort the *Keeper* to the city gates. Lock him out. If he tries to come back in, kill him."

"Yes, sir!"

The guards latched onto the Keeper and dragged him howling and screaming across the square and down the street, toward the gates. Along the way, the townsfolk closed in to watch. A few insulted the Keeper, and a few hurled rocks and sticks. Most stood silently by, wondering what this change would mean for them. They'd never had the strength or courage to fight the Keeper. They didn't have it for his cousin, either.

"I never did like him," the commander said as the Keeper vanished through the portcullis.

"Did you know about the god all along?" said River, gesturing at the broken machine.

The commander turned to face the steamscout. He reached out to touch it, feeling the warm metal under his hands. "I wanted to believe," he said. "My people... my father and his father before him... we all put our faith in this thing, and in the Keepers who controlled it. I always knew, though, at a certain level. Looking at the thing, I knew that it was made out of *parts*. I could see them. But somehow, I still feared that there was more to it... that somewhere inside all of that metal was truly a god."

"Your god was the Keeper," Socrates said. "A man, and nothing more."

"I see that now. I suspected it sometimes. I think most of us did. We couldn't risk saying anything, though. We were afraid of what might happen. Not just to us, but to our world. This is all we've ever known. I don't know what we'll do now."

"You'll see to your people," said Socrates. "Just as you always have."

The commander drew his gaze to the pyre and stared into the licking flames. Some of the townsfolk had closed in around them, and they stood watching him intently, waiting for his next command.

"We can't do this anymore," he said. "If we keep living like this, we'll all die."

"You don't need to," said Socrates. "We can teach you a better way."

The commander drew his shoulders back proudly and turned his gaze over the crowd that surrounded them. "Show me," he said to Socrates. "Explain everything."

The conversation lasted all night. The commander invited Socrates and his companions into the keep, where they gathered round the table and took turns telling Maru and the other townsfolk all about the world. Socrates and his crew explained steam engines and metallurgy to the commander. They told him about Starfall. They described the great city of Sanctuary and the strange and wonderful things in the world beyond the walls of the castle. They also told him about the Tal'mar and Vangars, and the trolls, the giants, and all the other aberrations of humanity they had encountered.

While they conversed, the guards and townspeople filled the room, listening intently to the strangers' stories, asking questions here and there, begging for more when it seemed that their visitors had finally run out of words. At some point, Micah appeared and begged the commander for his satchel. The commander immediately ordered the guards to return all of their personal possessions, and then graciously apologized for not doing so sooner. Micah thanked him profusely and then vanished back to his private attic in the train to sketch the memories that were still fresh in his mind.

As for the others, their conversation continued late into the night, until at last the light of dawn began creeping across the sky. Most of the townsfolk had long since returned to their homes and families, but a dozen or so remained, still intent and full of questions. In the end, it all came back to the commander's original question: *"What will happen to us now?"*

The citizens were confused and frightened. Some were even angry. No one could deny that they had all been fooled by the Keeper and his "god," and therefore they were cautious to speak out against the newcomers for fear of looking foolish again. The people had seen their god fall to the ground and break. Some had expected the clockwork god to rise up again, to cause fire to rain down from heaven and to cause men to fall down dead in their tracks. Instead, they had seen their Keeper come crawling out of the god's iron belly, injured and afraid.

With the collapse of their god, hundreds of years of reverence and tradition had come tumbling down. The people were uncertain. Their god had abandoned them, and they were frightened. Socrates knew it would not be easy to overcome all of that.

"I will see to the well first," Socrates announced as servants came in with breakfast. The room had slowly begun to fill with people, and as dawn broke, he once again found himself entertaining a full room. "I have devised a filtration system that will remove the Starfall from your water supply. This will prevent any more of you from becoming *Ancients*. It will also provide an energy source that you may use to heat your homes and to power machines.

"But we don't know how to do those things," the commander said. "We are simple, uneducated people."

"I will teach you what I can, and I will leave books to show you what I don't have time to explain. You must be patient. You must educate yourselves. You are capable of great things, but you must always have a thirst for knowledge. That is the only way to move forward. Do not simply replace your fallen god with another. You must always seek the truth."

"What of the Ancients?" someone in the crowd shouted. "What'll we do about them?"

"The Ancients will die, eventually. As distasteful as it sounds, you may be better off tackling the situation proactively."

"You mean killing them?" said the commander. He put an emphasis on the word *killing,* and he gave Socrates a meaningful look, reminding the simian of the delicate nature of the situation. The people of Blackstone had revered and worshipped the corpses of their ancestors for generations. Convincing them that it was now acceptable to kill the creatures would not be easy.

"Let's not be hasty," Socrates said wisely. "We must consider every avenue available to us."

Chapter 22

River, Socrates, and a few other crewmen joined forces that morning to build the town's new water filtration system. They were able to reclaim many useable parts from the steamscout, some of which they used to build the filter, the rest of which they loaded onto the train.

In the meanwhile, Burk and the rest of the crew who had abandoned Socrates very quietly returned to their duties. Socrates and River both noted this, but kept silent on the matter for the time being. They were focused on getting their job done, and had neither the energy nor the desire to stir the pot. Later, with the work done and the town of Blackstone safely behind them, would be the time for that confrontation.

Though she hadn't had any real sleep in two days, River threw herself into her work. She persisted at a frantic pace for the whole day, and her hard work paid off. By nightfall, the new filtration system was in place and it had already cleared several gallons of drinking water. A glass vial at the heart of the machine had slowly begun to capture the reclaimed Starfall, one drop at a time.

Later that night, over dinner, they finally discussed the future of Blackstone. It started when Kale asked how the commander would manage the city, now that the Keeper was gone.

"We'll have to elect a leader," the commander said.

"Better still, a council," Socrates advised. "Too much power should never rest in one man's hands."

"Sound advice. So it shall be done. I'll begin preparations tomorrow. By the end of the week, we should have new leadership in place. I hope that by then, we'll have a better idea of how to manage the situation with the Ancients."

That last statement sounded more like a question, and it seemed to be directed at Socrates. The automaton leaned back in his chair, the nearly silent clicking and whirring sounds drifting from his body like the sound of distant crickets.

"I'm afraid no answer I can give you would suffice," he said. "I don't know how long it will take for the Ancients to die off... at the moment I can't even guess how many there are. The one thing I know for sure is that your people can't go on the way they have been. They need nutrition that only the forest can provide. They need to build their strength back up if they're to survive."

"I understand," said the commander, "but I think you're overestimating these people. They have realized that they were tricked by the Keeper, but asking them to do this, to slay their own kin... they will not accept it."

"It isn't their kin," River said. "Don't they understand those people are dead already?"

"I'm afraid it's not that easy to dismiss a lifetime of belief," said the commander. "I've heard stories of your world. I can only imagine what it must be like. You grew up surrounded by different cultures; by people with beliefs and traditions very different from your own. You knew from childhood that there were many ways to view the world. It is not so with my people. Their ways are so ingrained into them that I fear they may not be able to change."

"They will over time," Socrates said. "The question is whether they will change fast enough to survive."

The conversation turned to other matters after that. Socrates promised to stay in the town for a few more days and have his crew educate the townsfolk on important matters such as farming and nutrition.

"My blacksmith can teach your men to harden iron into steel," he promised, "and to smelt ore from stones quarried in the hills nearby. Kale can teach your men to hunt wild game and to fish. River and I can show you how to make tools and build simple machines to make your lives easier-"

He was interrupted by a watch guard who came running down the stairs. "The Keeper!" the guard shouted breathlessly. "He's returned!"

"Where?" said the commander.

"The front gate, sir. He's blocked the portcullis!"

The commander leapt from his chair, spilling his wineglass across his dinner plate as he charged for the door. Socrates and the others jumped to their feet and hurried after him. The cool night air washed over them as they left the keep, fragrant with the odor of hearth fires and cooking dinners. The moon had risen to cast a silvery glow about the city. The group took little note of these facts as they raced out of the keep and down the street past the *Iron Horse,* finally stopping a few hundred yards from the front gate. Just as the guard had said, the portcullis was open. A dozen Ancients had already

found their way inside, and Townsfolk ran screaming past the group as the undead creatures lurched
after them.

"Guards, block the street!" the commander
shouted. "Turn over that wagon. Pull the furniture
out of those houses if you have to!"

"Oh, what a tragedy!" the Keeper's voice cried
out in feigned horror. A torch flared to life in the
darkness atop the wall, and the Keeper appeared.
There was a glint of madness in his eyes as he held
the torch aloft, waving it over the street. "It seems
you have forgotten the first rule of protecting
Blackstone, cousin. Always man the gate!"

"Madman!" the commander shouted. "What
have you done?"

"Nothing more than what you'd have done to
me," the Keeper snarled. He glanced down at the
guards piling up furniture before the horde of Ancients, and grinned menacingly. He hauled back the
torch and threw it. The flaming brand easily reached
its mark, and the overturned wagon immediately
burst into flames.

"Did you really think I could be exiled?" the
Keeper shouted. "Fools. I am your god! I will see you
all destroyed. This night, the plague of the dead will
take you all!"

The commander clenched his jaw. He stomped
across the street and yanked the crossbow out of a
guard's hands. He raised it, took half a second to
line up the sights, and released a bolt. "I'm your
god!" the Keeper shouted. "I will always rule over-"

With a thud, the crossbow bolt found home. The
Keeper's voice went silent and he stood there a
moment, swaying, staring down at the wooden shaft

projecting from his chest. With a gurgling sound, he toppled forward. His body landed in the street below with a heavy thump, and the Ancients instantly fell upon him.

As the Keeper's screams filled the night, the light of the fire illuminated the portcullis. Dozens... no, hundreds of Ancients pressed through the gate, clawing, moaning, slavering as they fought each other to get into the city. The flaming wagon had already crumbled, and as Socrates stood watching, the undead began making their way through the flames. They toppled forward, crawling over the burning wagon and piles of furniture, the fire licking at their flesh and bursting up from their ancient rotting clothes. Some fell to their hands and knees as their flesh gave way to the heat, but they continued to crawl, mindless of the searing flames or the stench of burning flesh rising from their bodies. Only when the heat became intense enough to destroy their brains did they finally collapse, but for every Ancient who fell, a dozen more appeared to fill the creature's place.

"We can't hold them," Kale shouted. "There are too many!"

"To the keep!" the commander ordered. "Everyone to the keep!"

"No!"

Socrates turned to face the commander and put his hand on the man's shoulder. "You have no food supply. You have no water stored. If you lock yourself in that keep, you'll all die in there."

"What, then?" the commander said. "What choice do we have?"

"Tell your people to board the train. I can carry you all to safety."

"But the Ancients-"

"The Ancients will tear your people apart if they stay here. They have your scent now, and they will wait you out. They never rest, and they never sleep."

The commander considered that, glancing back and forth between the horde of undead and the townspeople running for the safety of the keep.

"Don't take too long, commander."

Maru slumped his shoulders. "You're right. We cannot stay." The commander ran back up the street, calling out to his soldiers along the way. "Into the train! Guards, get everyone into the train. Hurry!"

Behind them, the firelight illuminated an endless stream of rotting corpses. They trailed out into the woods and filled the road beyond. The creatures had converged on the walls around the keep, and some of them had even managed to clamber up the trees and stones to the top of the wall. River appeared next to Socrates. The firelight danced in her eyes as she stared at the undead horde lumbering towards her.

"So many," she said softly. "Thousands of them..."

"Going back generations," Socrates said. "The Keeper has been to the graveyard. He brought them all here. He lured the Ancients into the city."

"Will the people be safe in the train?"

"Not here. We'll have to leave Blackstone."

"What about the Ancients? We can't just leave them like this. What if someone else were to come here?"

"No, we can't leave them," Socrates said. "I hope these people can someday forgive us for what we're about to do."

River turned to face him, and she became a silhouette against the backdrop of flames. "*What are we going to do, Socrates?*"

"Go to the train. Get your revolver, and go to the very last car. Wait until we're clear. Don't fail me. *And make sure no one sees you.*"

Socrates glanced over his shoulder towards the well, and River instantly understood. She broke into a run, pushing her way through the herd of evacuees near the train. Rather than fighting her way through the crowd, River leapt onto the front of the locomotive and raced down the narrow ledge, past the burners, to the engineer's platform. At the end of the platform, she launched herself across the gap onto the coal car. From there, she climbed onto the roof of the next railcar and broke into a sprint.

River sped down the roofline, leaping from car to car until the city wall rose up overhead. She ducked through the opening and leapt easily to the roof of the next car. Beyond the castle wall, a narrow steel bridge crossed a steep ravine, and she glanced uneasily at the tiny metal structure supporting the massive train hundreds of feet in the air. The land below was dark, but she knew well that it was cluttered with boulders and strewn with broken trees. One slip or a heavy gust of wind would be enough to send her plummeting to her death.

So high, she thought anxiously, the blood draining from her face. *Why is it always heights?*

River's heart thudded in her ears, and for a moment she completely forgot her mission. She stood at the edge of the railcar, gazing down at that black abyss, and suddenly realized she was shaking. River clenched her fists and closed her eyes, trying to ignore the sensation she was feeling. As her body temperature dropped, her adrenaline surged. River almost felt like her body was not her own; as if it might not respond to her will, and if she took a single step she might just tumble over the edge.

Beyond the bridge, the *Iron Horse* weaved back and forth until it disappeared under the heavy woodland canopy. Behind her, inside the city's walls, River heard a small explosion of musket fire. Some of the crew had begun to fire on the Ancients. She grimaced, thinking of Socrates. He most certainly wouldn't have allowed that. Someone must have disobeyed his orders. That wasn't a good sign.

These thoughts brought her senses back to reality. River opened her eyes and gazed at the train stretching into the woods ahead. "Just run," she said quietly. "It's just a straight line, just RUN!"

River ducked her head low and broke into a sprint, racing toward the far side of the bridge. She reached the end of the railcar and leapt, telling herself not to look down into that black gap, but she did it anyway. The sight brought a surge of fear that rolled up and down her body and very nearly caused her to stumble. River suppressed the feeling. She landed on the next railcar and continued running, forcing herself to focus on the trees ahead.

She leapt from that car to the next, and then again, until at last the ground rose up to meet the tracks, and the irrational panic that had a hold on her slowly gave way to relief. The bridge ended and she paused a moment to catch her breath. She turned back, gazing across the chasm to where the train disappeared inside the castle wall. The orange glow of fires made a halo in the smoke-filled sky over Blackstone, and she heard voices shouting in the distance. River hadn't heard any more musket fire. Hopefully that meant Socrates had managed to regain control of the crew.

The sound of the train's whistle cut through the night and River knew that Socrates was prepping the massive steam engine for departure. With any luck, the last of the townsfolk were now boarding. It occurred to her that the sound of the whistle might attract the undead, and she realized that was probably what Socrates had intended. He was drawing them to the train, getting them all as close as possible to the heart of the city.

That thought spurred her back into action. River broke into a run. She crossed the next three railcar roofs and, on the third, paused to stoop over and pull open an access door. She dropped through the hatch and landed in the hallway next to her private compartment. River rushed inside and quickly located her revolver hanging on the wall. With practiced efficiency, she strapped on her gun belt and then raced back into the hallway to climb back onto the roof.

River leapt up, caught the rim of the hatch, and pulled herself quickly to the roof. As she cleared the opening, she glimpsed a shadow moving on the roof next to her. She twisted her head around just in time to catch the buttstock of a crossbow on her forehead. River threw her head back, but not quickly enough to avoid the blow. She reeled, falling backwards across the railcar roof. A dark shadow loomed over her and she looked up into Commander Toolume's face.

"Sorry about this," Maru said grimly as he aimed the crossbow at her chest. "But I can't let you do what you're planning to do."

Chapter 23

"I never should have let you into my town," the commander said. "I should have shot Kale down in the road the night I first saw him. Then none of this would have happened."

River put a hand to her forehead and wiped away a trickle of blood. She glanced at the warm crimson fluid on her fingertips and then wiped it on her leather breeches. She glanced up the train, past him, and found they that were alone. Her mind worked frantically, putting together the pieces.

"Why are you doing this?" she said. "We're only trying to help you!"

"I tried to tell you. I tried to explain but Socrates wouldn't listen. I won't let you destroy us like this. You should have just left us. You should never have come."

"I don't understand. What is it you want? You want to go back to the way it was? Watching your people slowly starve and die, trapped in that castle?"

"At least we knew what we were doing," he said. "We had a god. We knew right from wrong."

"But you didn't! You must see that now. The things you were doing weren't right."

"Subjective," he said dismissively. "None of it matters now, regardless. Nothing will ever be the same. At least I can live up to my oath. I can protect my people, and the Ancients. Then they will still accept me as the Keeper."

River closed her eyes and sighed. Of all the people in Blackstone, the commander had seemed most ready to accept a new way of life. She realized now that he hadn't been as open about his feelings as he'd led them to believe.

"I thought you wanted to change things. I thought you wanted a better life. Or was that all just talk, to get us to leave?"

"Oh, I wanted things to change. I wanted my cousin dead. I wanted to proclaim myself the lord of this city and put things to right... I couldn't do that until you left, though. You're right about that. I suppose I could have let you and the others burn on that pyre, but then I'd have had your crew to deal with. And your train, of course, which would serve as a constant reminder and temptation to the others. So many variables to deal with. All I really wanted was for you to be gone. That's why I saved you. So you could get on your train and get the hell out of my city."

River stared up at him, noting his finger on the crossbow's trigger. She moved her arm slightly, wondering if she could possibly reach her revolver. The commander responded by pressing the crossbow bolt into her chest. The sharpened steel tip bit into her flesh and her lips parted.

"Don't even try it," he said.

A trickle of blood ran down River's sweat-moistened flesh, and his glance strayed to her bosoms, straining against her bodice. River felt the heat of his lusty gaze lingering there. She cocked an eyebrow.

"See something you like, Commander?"

He yanked his gaze away from her cleavage and fixed her with a menacing stare. "If you were one of my servants, I'd rape you for that."

The steam whistle howled in the distance, and River felt a gentle tug against the car beneath her. The distant hiss of steam told her Socrates had released the brakes.

"Is that what you like, raping girls?" she said, staring into his face. She slid her hand up to pull the strings on her bodice, loosening the knot. The leather parted, spreading wide to reveal the pale cleavage between her breasts. The commander narrowed his eyes.

"What are you playing at?" he said quietly.

"Don't you like to play, Commander? Don't you want to tell me what to do? Don't you want to *hurt me?*"

He licked his lips and cast a wary glance over his shoulder, verifying that they were still alone. River tugged the strings, parting her bodice, almost fully revealing her breasts. "You'd better hurry up, commander," she said teasingly. "We don't have all day. *Hurt me.*"

That was all he could take. He set his crossbow off to the side and bent over her, dropping to one knee. He squeezed her breast in his right hand, and when she didn't resist, he bent closer. A moan escaped his lips. River smiled and reached up, drawing him in, parting her lips for a kiss.

An instant before they touched, she jerked her head forward, slamming her forehead in to his nose. The commander reeled back, cursing, scrambling blindly for the crossbow off to his side. River kicked at it, knocking the weapon out of reach. It clattered across the metal roof. The commander turned aside and lunged after his weapon, but it slid over the edge of the roof and disappeared into the forest underbrush.

In an instant, River was on her feet. The commander cursed as he realized she'd tricked him. He lunged at her, but she already had her pistol in hand. She leveled it at his face and smiled coldly. He wiped the blood from his nose and spat.

"Blood for blood," she said, her finger dancing on the trigger. "Step back." He sized her up for a moment and then reluctantly took a step back.

"Good," she said, nodding at the hatch next to him. "Now open that door and get in."

The commander bent over the hatch and pulled it open. He glanced inside and then fixed her with a furious glare. "You'll live to regret this," he said.

"You're lucky I'm letting *you* live at all. Get in."

Suddenly the train lurched forward. The engine had engaged at full power, and the railcar seemed to jump under River's feet. She lost her footing and her legs went out from under her. She dropped flat on her back. Instantly, the commander was upon her. River tried to raise the pistol, but he caught her by the wrist and slammed her hand into the roof. A painful spasm shot up and down her arm and the revolver slid from her grip. Maru snatched it up and tossed it through the open hatch. River winced as it vanished.

"Let's put that collar of yours to good use," the commander said. He raised his fist and punched her solidly on the cheek. River's head snapped back, slamming into the railcar. Stars exploded in her vision. She clenched her fists, struggling to bring her

201

reeling mind back into focus, desperately clinging to consciousness. River knew if she blacked out now, she'd never wake up.

The commander still had a firm grasp on her right hand, but her left was free. She struck at him, landing a solid right hook on his temple. The sudden attack caught him by surprise, and River took advantage by swinging again as fast as she could. The second blow went wide, grazing his ear. She swung again.

Caught off guard by the ferocity of her attack, the commander threw his arm out, struggling to block her blows. His grip on her wrist relaxed, and River took advantage. She lifted her arm and yanked him forward, pulling him off balance. As he came within reach, she slammed her forehead forward, once again crushing his nose under her skull. This time the cartilage collapsed and his nose was completely smashed. An involuntary roar erupted from his mouth as blood sprayed out of his nostrils. His hands went to his face.

River swung her head to the side, trying to avoid the spray of blood. She struck out at him with both fists, slamming them into the commander's chest with all her strength. The impact knocked him backwards. He rolled sideways and came up in a crawling position as she struggled to get back on her feet.

"You're dead!" he shouted through the blood. "I'm going to rip your head off, whore!"

He lunged at her, and River danced back. She was dazed. She moved slower than she meant to and somehow he managed to latch onto her boot. He gave her a yank and River dropped to the roof. She scrambled back frantically, but he held fast. Instinctively, River kicked at him with her free leg. She landed a solid blow to the side of his head and the commander lost his grip. He rolled sideways, moaning as he clutched at his head. Blood ran freely from his nose and smeared the steel roof around him, slickening the surface.

For a moment, the battle seemed to be over. River crawled to her feet and leapt toward the hatch. Unfortunately, the commander managed to get to his knees and throw himself in her path. She twisted out of reach as he lunged for her, and she took a step backwards. The commander's right hand snaked around his back, and a long dagger appeared.

"That's enough playing," he said hoarsely.

River danced back as he swung the blade at her. The glimmering steel whistled through the air, missing her throat by a fraction of an inch. Her gaze flitted back and forth from his face to the dagger, and to the open hatch just a few feet beyond. Over his shoulder, the castle came into view. She was running out of time.

River lunged at the commander, trying to draw the older man into an attack and force him off balance. He swung at her, but with minimal effort. He was too clever to be fooled by that trick. He pressed forward, brandishing the dagger menacingly, and an evil laugh erupted from his throat. River had no choice but to take a step back, putting even more distance between herself and the hatch.

"Keep going," the commander said. "Keep walking. Sooner or later, you're gonna run out of train." He wiped his face with the back of his sleeve and smeared blood over the fabric. Gooey black and crimson clots dribbled down over his lips and across his chin. River's stomach churned at the sight.

He was right, she realized. It would be hard enough to jump to the next railcar while avoiding that knife. What would happen when she reached the end of the train? He'd kill her, that was what. He'd rape her and then slit her throat and toss her over the rails. By then, they'd be inside the city and she'd be food for the Ancients.

River glanced over the edge of the roof, and contemplated leaping into the ravine. She wouldn't survive the fall but at least it would be quick. Somehow, it wasn't as frightening as before.

River heard a strange whirring sound and glanced over the commander's shoulder. He took no note of the noise, instead lunging forward with another attack. River dodged. As she moved aside, she saw a lightning flash of steel; a metal ball the size of her thumb barreling through the air so fast it was hardly even visible. River had a fraction of a second to recognize the shape of a crude musket ball before it plunged into the back of the commander's skull. He froze, mid-step, and the knife slipped from his grasp. It clattered to the metal roof and skittered off the edge. River stared at the commander, too shocked to move.

His eyes rolled back in his head and he dropped forward, nearly crashing into her. River stepped aside, allowing Maru's body to drop to the railcar. Blood poured out of his skull and his limbs twitched uncontrollably for a few seconds. At last, he went perfectly still. River looked up to see Thane standing on the roof at the end of the next car. She stared at him, her mouth agape. He wasn't carrying a musket, or any other firearm that she could see. How could he possibly have thrown that steel ball so powerfully?

"What did you do?"

"Sling," he explained, holding up a long leather thong. He leapt the gap between railcars and hurried to her side. "It's the only weapon I ever could seem to use right."

"Thanks," she said somewhat awkwardly. She was still dazed from the fight, and slightly in shock from its sudden resolution.

"My pleasure," Thane said.

He nudged the commander's body with his boot, and the lifeless corpse slid over the edge of the railcar and plunged into the ravine below. River's eyes widened as she realized they were entering the castle.

"My gun!" she said, leaping for the hatch. "I have to get to the back of the train."

"Ah, one thing," Thane said awkwardly, eyeing her exposed breasts. River glanced down.

"Oh!" she said, reaching for her bodice. "Sorry!"

"No, sweetness," Thane said with a laugh. "Never, ever apologize for that."

He winked at her and River blushed as she yanked the strings tight. She wordlessly dropped through the hatch, vanishing into the car below. Thane stared after her for a moment, smiling.

River blinked, trying to adjust her vision to the darkness inside the railcar. She turned and caught a glimpse of the town square passing by through the window. Awkward, lumbering shapes moved about in the silvery moonlight. She saw them straggling, crawling, reaching for the train. She saw their horrid disjointed faces and gleaming skulls; saw them tripping and tumbling under the wheels of the train to be crushed against the unyielding iron tracks.

Horrified, she drew her gaze away. A glint of brass caught her eye and she snatched up her weapon, instinctively shoving it back into the holster on her hip. River broke into a run, flying down the hall and out the door, pausing only long enough to turn the handle as she entered the next car. Running at full tilt, she barely spared a glance at the contents of the railcars around her. She sped through tunnel-like hallways and broad, empty cars, leaping over piles of stored goods and mechanical odds and ends.

Through the windows, she caught glimpses of the town square and knew that, if nothing else, she was at least matching the train's speed. Unfortunately, the *Iron Horse* was gaining speed with every passing second, and River couldn't run any faster. She tore through another door, nearly ripping it off the hinges, and at last found herself at the end of the train. She reached for the handle and her heart sank as it held firm in her grasp. The door was locked.

River glanced outside and saw the keep to her right, and the town square stretching out behind her. She saw the dark looming shapes filling the area like a swarm of ants over a picnic. Desperately, she kicked at the door, trying to break it free. It was made of steel, and the lock held. Frustrated, River drew her revolver and shot the lock. It bent inward, so she kicked the door again. Still, it held.

Through the window, she glimpsed the city well and the water filter sitting at the edge of the square.

She recognized the bluish glow of Starfall inside the water filter, and saw that it was fading fast into the distance. She had to act. She had one chance to destroy the Starfall and all the Ancients at once, but that moment was quickly passing.

River glanced around and realized she had overlooked the most obvious escape. She raised her weapon and fired into one of the train's windows, averting her eyes as the glass exploded around her. River used the barrel of her revolver to knock the rest of the glass out and then climbed through. The tiny shards that remained in the window frame cut her hands and arms, but she ignored the razor-like slices and forced her way through. With blood streaming from the palms of her hands and down her shoulders, she reached for the framing over the back platform and swung herself around. With a light *thud,* she landed on the platform. River raised her pistol and aligned the sights on the vial of Starfall a hundred yards back. And it vanished.

"No," she said in a half-whisper. The undead creatures had closed in around the well, all but concealing it from her, making it impossible to shoot the vial of Starfall. Even if she could tell where it was, which she couldn't, she still couldn't shoot through all those bodies.

Don't fail me, Socrates' voice said in her head. She knew exactly what it meant. They had one chance to do this, and they'd never get another. Despite everything she had done, River had done just that. She had failed.

"No," she said again, this time firmer. "It's not over yet."

River crawled on the handrail at the edge of the platform and leapt in the air, catching the corner of the roof. She grunted as she heaved herself up, kicking her feet, swaying side to side for a perch. River caught one of the brass bars that lined the roof and pulled herself up and over. She instantly leapt to her feet and raised her pistol. The last railcar had already reached the far castle wall, and the water filter was but a tiny target in the distance.

She frowned, peering down the sights, trying to catch a glimpse of the bluish glow of Starfall. Through the press of bodies, she saw a flash of light. River squeezed the trigger. She grimaced as a spark glanced off the upper framing of the pump. River steadied herself, took another deep breath, and fired again.

The second shot missed as well, but she did manage to strike one of the undead creatures in the head. The thing toppled backwards, landing on the body next to it, and they both fell to the ground. In that instant, River saw the familiar glow of the vial, clear as day. She lined up sights and caught her breath, calculating the distance and the arc of the bullet's flight. She adjusted her aim, twelve inches high and a bit to the left... Then she squeezed the trigger.

The round struck home with an instant eruption. Bright blue-green light filled the square and expanded out through the town in a shockwave, hurtling bodies into the air and flattening buildings as it rolled outward. The massive inferno of color pushed into the sky, licking at the heavens even as it spread through the town, toppling or destroying everything in its path.

River lost sight of the explosion for a second as The *Iron Horse* slid effortlessly through the outer wall and into the forest beyond. Even outside the wall, the shockwave still hit River so hard it knocked her down. She landed on her back and lay there, struggling to catch her breath, watching bits and pieces of burning buildings float through the heavens like fiery stars. As the last light of the explosion faded to a glow in the distance, they began raining down.

River pushed to her feet and found Thane standing next to her. He caught her by the arm and helped steady her balance. River looked into the bard's sharp, playful gaze and felt a sudden irrepressible urge to kiss him. She wasn't sure why. Perhaps it was the way that he had saved her with his sling, or perhaps it was the sudden relief she felt and the fact that he just happened to be there... and happened to be quite good looking, at that.

Then she remembered standing bare-breasted in front of him only a few moments earlier and her passion melted into embarrassment. She pulled away, and gave him an appreciative smile.

"I have to tell Socrates," she mumbled, and headed for the nearest roof hatch.

Chapter 24

The Great Iron Horse pulled to a complete stop fifty miles outside of Blackstone. In that time, the forest had grown dense and impassable, forcing the *Horse* to plow through the terrain, clearing a path as it rolled onward. The inhabitants of the city huddled in the railcars, fearful and wondering, unsure as to what might become of them now that their city was gone. For there could be no doubt: Blackstone had been utterly destroyed.

The forest outside dwindled away to scrub brush and wild grain, and eventually gave way to broad rolling steppes, foreboding but brimming with life. Here, the Wastelands finally succumbed, and the last patchy remnants of snow faded into vast plains of green. Socrates locked the brakes and the *Horse* rolled to a stop. Over the intercom, he ordered the crew to guide the citizens of Blackstone out of the train so he could address them all in person. An icy cold wind blew across the steppes as they gathered, two hundred families in all. Men tried to console their wives and mothers their children. In hushed voices, they praised Socrates and cursed him all at once.

"Will he abandon us here to starve and die?" some wondered. "Or will he force us to join his crew and make us into slaves?"

Ultimately of course, no one knew his mind but Socrates. They watched in silence as he clambered up the front of the locomotive and stood on the narrow brass rail along the burners. He gazed down on them, a strange amalgamation of beast and machine that spoke like a man, and held over them the power of a god. In silence he gazed at them, patient, thoughtful, until at last, he finally spoke:

"Good people of Blackstone, I stand before you a humble machine, begging your forgiveness. I had no right to invade your world. I had no wish to see your god fall or your Ancients destroyed. My only wish was to rejoin my companions and pursue our quest into the great wilds of the world. Alas, despite the best of intentions, this was not to be.

"For those of you who did not witness the end, I can assure you that your city has been destroyed. Your homes are gone and the castle of your ancestors lies in ruins. Still, all is not without hope. Should you so wish it, I can return you there and help to rebuild the filter in your well. I can show you how to rebuild Blackstone better than it ever was. But I must warn you, this path will be fraught with difficulty and danger.

"Alternatively, you are welcome to join my crew. I can carry you to the next city and leave you there if you so choose, or you may find a permanent home aboard the *Iron Horse,* and join us on our quest for adventure. I leave this decision up to you. We will rest here for one day while you decide."

With that, Socrates stepped back onto the locomotive platform and stealthily made his way back into the train. Behind him, voices rose in a clamor.

The arguing went on for hours. Some were anxious to return to their homes, while others argued that this wasn't even possible. Some called for Socrates' head while others countered that if not for him, they'd have been trapped and killed by the Ancients. After all, it was the Keeper who had betrayed them, not Socrates.

They argued deep into the night, until at last they decided to rest and consider their positions. Tomorrow, they would vote.

In the end, the people of Blackstone decided to stay with Socrates and his crew. Those few who argued for a return soon realized that they would be alone, and woefully ill-equipped for success. Survival, they realized, was more important. By noon the next day, the *Iron Horse* was rolling down the tracks toward destinies unknown.

That evening, River, Kale, and the others assembled in the dining car for a few drinks and a friendly game of cards. River tried bluffing her way through the first hand, but lost her concentration as Shayla settled onto a stool behind Kale and began stroking his hair and tickling his earlobes. It wasn't the woman's attention that distracted River so much as the warrior's reaction. Kale, an incorrigible ladies' man, actually blushed!

River wasn't sure what it was about this that unsettled her so, or what it was about the attractive auburn-haired woman that put her so on edge. She tried to ignore the uneasy churning in the pit of her stomach, but it was futile. She played out of the second hand within minutes, and by the third hand had lost more coinage than she cared to remember.

"I'm out," she said as Thane started dealing the next hand of cards. He gave her a gentle smile.

"Are you sure, sweetness? I would be happy to cover your losses."

River felt a moment of elation as she saw Kale arch an eyebrow, and his gaze drifted back and forth between them. Thane's smile was tempting, as was his offer, but...

"No, thank you," she said at last. "I haven't slept in days. I think I'll turn in."

She saw something in Thane's smile, a question or perhaps an offer, but she rose from her chair and turned away without a response. Thane was enticing, but River was nowhere near giving in to him. Not yet. Especially not after what had happened on the roof of the train that afternoon. It was bad enough that he had her at a disadvantage; worse still that he'd had to save her. If there was one thing River couldn't abide, it was helplessness. Especially when she saw it in herself.

She settled her tab at the bar and left, wandering back through the cars until she happened to bump into Socrates outside the lab. For a machine, he looked strangely tired. The folds of skin around his eyes seemed dark and baggy, and his eyes were slightly bloodshot. River stared at him in surprise.

"Socrates!" she said. "Sorry, I didn't realize-"

"No worries," he said. "I'm on my way to the library for some rest."

River leaned forward, frowning as she gazed into his eyes.

"Socrates, do you sleep?"

He considered her question a moment. "I suppose you could say that I do. I am an automaton of course, but my internal mechanisms require cooling and maintenance. If I were to run at full speed day and night... well, I'm sure you can imagine."

"I can," River agreed. "In fact, I think it's happening to me right now."

"Indeed. Until tomorrow, then..."

"Socrates, wait! I... I need to tell you something."

He frowned, gazing into her eyes with an almost human expression of concern. "What is it?"

"I owe you an apology. When I left the other day, against your orders... I had been talking to Burk, and some of the others, and I'm afraid I doubted your judgment. I'm not sure why. I've never seen anything in you but genius, but I started to wonder if..."

"If you could trust a machine?"

River averted her gaze. "I suppose so, yes. For a while there, I wasn't sure if you really knew... I wasn't sure you could *feel*."

"Well, I *am* a machine. That fact is incontrovertible. Is this going to be a problem for you?"

"No, of course not! I knew right away that I'd made a mistake. Unfortunately, we were already up to our necks in trouble at that point. But I knew it was a mistake, and I'm sorry."

"Say no more. I understand entirely."

"So you forgive me?"

Socrates laughed. It was the first time in days that River had heard the deep rumbling sound that came rolling out of his barrel-sized chest, and she couldn't help but smile.

"Go to bed, child," he said. "Speak no more of this silliness."

He disappeared through the doorway and River found herself alone, accompanied only by the sound of the rails and the vibration of the train beneath her feet. With a sigh, she turned to make the trek back to her private quarters.

Not far away, Socrates found Burk. He was standing on the platform outside the dining car, nursing the last few drops of a bottle of rum. He was accompanied by two workers, one a broad-should-ered human who had been a Blackstone guardsman, the other a Tal'mar half-elf with a reputation for thievery. They all stiffened as Socrates appeared.

"Burk, I'd like a word with you," Socrates said.

Burk shrugged and his companions obediently vanished inside the dining car. Once they were alone, Burk gulped down the last swallow and tossed his bottle over the rail. The sound of breaking glass vanished in the distance.

"Well, what is it?" Burk demanded, leaning over Socrates as if to demonstrate his massive bulk.

Socrates looked up into Burk's face, gauging the man's mood. He was drunk; belligerent. He was eager to prove his superiority to this creature that was half his size. Somehow, in Burk's mind, his domineering size and strength made him superior to the simian creation. Socrates identified this as one of several problems that needed immediate remedy.

Socrates threw out a long, sinewy arm and caught Burk by the throat. Burk's hands instinctively went to the gorilla's arm, trying to fend off the attack. As Burk's hands closed around Socrates' forearm, the ape lifted the blacksmith off the ground. Then, with all the agility and raw power of a wild untamed beast, Socrates leapt to the handrail and caught the ladder in one hand. In the other, he dragged the massive blacksmith along. Almost instantaneously, they were atop the dining car.

Socrates stretched his arm out over the edge of the train, dangling Burk over the darkness by the neck. The entire event was so fluid and fast that Burk didn't even realize what had happened until everything stopped. Then, too late, he realized his precarious situation. All Socrates had to do was let go, and Burk would be little more than a bloody spot along the rails, thousands of miles from nowhere.

"What are you doing?" Burk said in a raspy, choking voice. He clutched desperately at Socrates' arm, hoping at least that might save him if the ape released his grip.

"I said we'd have a talk," Socrates growled. "What I meant was that *I* will talk, and *you* will listen."

Burk nodded desperately, his eyes wild with terror.

"Good. We have reached a crossroads, you and I. I'm afraid that if we press on, one of us might not survive." As if to accentuate his point, Socrates tightened his grip on Burk's throat.

"Yes, yes," the blacksmith coughed. "I understand."

"Your actions over the last few days have endangered me, along with the rest of the crew. You have endangered our mission and you have endangered *my train*. Do you understand what I'm saying?"

Burk nodded desperately.

"Excellent. Now, I understand that you're not the sharpest sword in the armory, so let me phrase this as succinctly as possible: should you ever endanger my crew or my mission again, I will tear your arms off and feed them to the undead corpses that roam the forest outside Blackstone Castle. Then, while you're still alive, I'll chain you to the plow on the front of my train and use you as a battering ram for the next thousand miles. Whatever's left of you after that, I'll toss alongside the rails as food for the vultures, rats, and the other starving creatures of the world more deserving of a meal than you are of life. Do you understand me?"

"Yes," Burk grunted breathlessly. "Yes, sir!"

"Good."

Socrates twisted aside, tossing Burk to the roof of the railcar. The large man tumbled a few feet and rolled to a stop, clutching wildly at the rail as he nearly rolled over the edge. Socrates took a step towards him, and Burk flinched.

"I'm glad we had this talk," Socrates snarled. "Let's not have another." With that, he turned away and vanished over the edge of the car.

Burk sat alone in the darkness, rubbing his throat and listening to the sounds of laughter and music drifting up from the dining car below. At last, he pushed to his feet and drunkenly staggered toward the ladder.

"Gonna kill me an ape," he whispered to the icy wind, and stared up at the stars spinning overhead.

THE END

217

A word from the author:

Thank you for reading "The Clockwork God." I hope you enjoyed reading this story as much as I enjoyed writing it. Book Two in the series is available now. If you enjoy my books, please post a review and tell a friend! Your reviews at Amazon.com and other retailers are invaluable, not only to me, but also to other readers who are looking for their next book.

Also, visit my website and sign up for my newsletter if you want the latest news on upcoming books, contests, and giveaways. Thanks again!

www.jamiesedgwick.com